Alex has already lost one lover to his brother Zeca. Now his fickle shenanigans have driven Hugh, his other lover, away as well. Alex desperately wants what his brother has, an intensely passionate relationship, so Zeca shares their father's advice — you have to love before you can be relentless. Good advice, if Alex weren't so afraid to follow it.

When Toppy's own love life gets a little, um . . . strange, he escapes to St. Tropez. He takes Alex with him, who finds himself face-to-face with Hugh. Too bad Hugh is already lip-to-lip with someone else. But Alex has come too far to turn back now.

The game is on, and while Toppy gets up to his own sexual shenanigans under the St. Tropez sun, Alex will do anything to get back into Hugh's life . . . his bed . . . his body. He'll first have to learn to face his fears. Only then can he find relentless love.

This book has been previously published.

Relentless Love
Copyright © 2019 A.J. Llewellyn
ISBN: 978-1-4874-2496-1
Cover art by Martine Jardin

Published by eXtasy Books Inc or
Devine Destinies, an imprint of eXtasy Books Inc

Look for us online at:
www.eXtasybooks.com or www.devinedestinies.com

Relentless Love
Relentless Book 2

By

A.J. Llewellyn

DEDICATION

Dedicated to my high school teacher Miss Thomas, who told her class one day that she was torn between two lovers. Thanks for the idea, and the knowledge that the quest for true love must be relentless.

TRADEMARKS ACKNOWLEDGEMENT

The author acknowledges the trademarked status and trademark owners of the following wordmarks mentioned in this work of fiction:

BAFTA: British Academy of Film and Television Arts
Boss: HUGO BOSS Trade Mark Management GmbH & Co. KG
Brigadoon: Metro-Goldwyn-Mayer
Café de Paris: 25 Rue Saffren, Saint-Tropez
Chez Maggy: 7 Rue Sibille, Saint-Tropez
Chrysler Sebring: FCA US LLC
Don't You Want Me: written by Jo Callis, Phillip Oakley, Phillip Adrian Wright
eBay: eBay Inc.
Hotel Lou Cagnard: Hotel Lou Cagnard St-Tropez
I Get Along Without You Very Well: music by Hoagy Carmichael, lyrics Jane Brown Thompson
It's Bad For Me: written by Cole Porter
Jacuzzi: Jacuzzi, Inc.
Lady Gaga: Ate My Heart Inc.
Levi's: Levi Strauss & Co.
Mean Girls: Paramount Pictures
Mercedes E350 Cabriolet: Daimler AG Corporation
Tom Ford: Ford, Thomas C. Individual United States
Triumph: Bayerische Motoren Werke AG
Water for Elephants: written by Sara Gruen

CHAPTER ONE

M an oh man, it was sickening. Was such passion in the
early hours of the morning even normal? I wiped
down the countertop inside my dad's restaurant, watching
my brother Zeca kissing his boyfriend Antonio goodbye.
Their frenzied kisses attracted not only *my* attention but that
of a few passersby. The way they went at each other, anyone
would think they were about to be separated for months,
years even—not just the few hours my brother worked until
Antonio sloped back into our café for his late-morning
coffee.

Sheesh. I checked my watch. In one minute I would have a
legitimate gripe. I could accuse my brother of being late. I
watched the hungry way the two men gnawed at each other's mouths. Antonio and Zeca were as predictable as Swiss
clocks, and a thousand times more ardent than any other
lovers I knew, gay or straight.

They stood in the doorway of Café Toppy, our father's
famous restaurant in the heart of Capri. They broke off their
kiss, gasping for breath. Antonio looked up and down the
street, his hand moving surreptitiously to Zeca's ass. A little
squeeze and he pulled Zeca closer to him.

Oh brother.

I moved past our stocked shelves of lemon-flavored liqueurs, spice rubs, and teas, prickles of fury forming along
the back of my neck. Did they have to make such a spectacle
of themselves?

Zeca broke off their kiss again, glancing at me then back

1

at his lover. Antonio took Zeca's face in his hands and tugged my brother toward him for a longer, deeper kiss.

Oh, for corn's sake.

I brushed past them, broom in hand, and made a big display of cleaning up out front. Antonio finally let my brother go, giving me a finger wave.

"*Ciao*, Alex."

He took off down the street. He had a sexy swagger, I'll give him that. My brother watched him for a moment, a loopy grin on his face.

"*Buongiorno!*" he shouted, waving at a few store owners who were also gearing up for a busy morning.

Good? What was good about it?

Via Camerelle, the main promenade of Capri was kicking into high gear and it was barely seven o'clock. The Christmas and New Year season was over, the remaining holiday tourists now jostling for space with serious professional travelers. They came here year after year, stayed at the same hotels or villas, ate the same meals each and every time . . . and spent *a lot* of money.

Zeca drifted into the café, a dreamy expression on his face, and began warming up the cappuccino machine. Since nailing the sexiest guy on the island, my twin's fortunes had changed. I still couldn't believe it. Antonio had been *my* boyfriend until I'd made the colossal mistake of asking Zeca to pose as me for a date. I'd met another guy and wanted to give Hugh a chance. I have no idea how it all went so wrong, but I'd found myself attracted to Hugh, my married next-door neighbor — to a woman, no less, which really shows you how screwed up I was — *and* Antonio.

Antonio figured out the ruse after a couple of dates with my brother. Maybe I'd miscalculated, considering Antonio's a cop. I should have guessed he'd be smarter than the guys I usually went for.

Zeca was humming a song, smiling at me. Couldn't he see me frowning at him? Couldn't he feel my death-ray stare?

He strolled into the kitchen and began chopping vegetables. Our winter menu was still in full force, and he didn't seem to mind the grunt work of chopping all those hearty root vegetables. Me, I hated chopping, slicing, and cooking. I hated anything to do with food in fact, except for eating it.

The smell of lemons was strong. Damn lemons. I couldn't escape them on Capri, and they always reminded me of Hugh and the last meal we had together. It should have been the most romantic meal of our lives—

Stop it. Don't think about it.

I finished putting tables and chairs out front. I caught the gaze of the woman next door who owned the chocolate shop. *Oh, God.* She was setting up a new window display of red and pink hearts. Valentine's Day. *Holy moly.* It was just around the corner, and I was the only guy on Capri who didn't have a Valentine. I thought about Hugh. The thought of his wonderful kisses and how much I missed them almost ruined me.

For a moment I stood leaning on the broom handle. The sun was peeping through the big, puffy clouds, like a yolk in a sea of poached egg whites. Even winter in Capri was gorgeous. I could hear Zeca's rhythmic chopping coming from the kitchen and detected a whiff of onions. With a huge sigh, I went back inside and tucked the broom behind the kitchen door.

Zeca glanced up at me and beamed. He was so fucking happy these days, it was disgusting. I hardly saw him anymore, since he spent all his nights with Antonio. They spent every spare second together and seemed closer each day. I'd never heard them argue, never heard Zeca say one bad thing about Antonio. As for Antonio, he also seemed smitten. It was aggravating. *Aggravating!*

"Don't you ever get sick of him?" I asked.

Zeca scooped up handfuls of onions and swept them into a plastic bowl. "Sick of Antonio?" His hands stopped mid-air, a torrent of chopped onions falling between his fingers. That was another thing that bugged me. He chopped vegetables so bloody evenly. "No. Never." Zeca frowned. "Why would you even ask me a question like that?"

"You've been with him practically forever—"

"Two months," he interjected, an exasperated look on his face.

"Exactly." I pointed at him. "Don't you yearn for . . . a bit of variety?"

He stared at me, open-mouthed. He broke into a cheeky grin. "Oh, we have variety."

"You're talking about sexual positions. I'm talking about the man himself. Don't you ever want to kiss a total stranger?"

"What? No!"

He washed and wiped the chef's knife and began working on sweet chili peppers. His rhythm was off, however. I'd gotten to him. I don't know why, but I got a sick little thrill out of that.

"Is this about Hugh?" my brother asked, breaking his own stride. He placed the knife on the chopping board and stared at me again.

"No." I swallowed hard. Things were weird between me and Hugh. I had feelings for the guy. I just didn't know what they were.

"No?" Zeca arched a brow at me.

"Not really." I kicked at the doorframe. My brother knew me too well. Hugh had jumped off his cruise ship to come back to me when he was supposed to leave. He'd braved sharks and everything. It was the most romantic thing that had ever happened to me . . . but I was also embroiled with Mrs. Pampina at the time. My cheeks flushed with shame just thinking about it. I had gone back and forth between them, with ghastly results.

"You could go visit him you know, or maybe invite him back here." Zeca's tone was soft.

"No." My heart had hardened to Hugh. Whenever I thought of him, I was reminded of my foolish escapade with Mrs. Pampina. I'd always enjoyed having more than one lover at a time. When things got too serious with one, I'd hop to the other flower, like a drunken, dizzy bee. But when things went pear-shaped with Mrs. Pampina, Hugh got all territorial on me. I was supposed to explain my every move to him. I was supposed to be available. We argued, he shouted, and two weeks ago, we'd had a very bad argument, and he'd left the island in a huff.

For several days I'd thought he'd return, but he didn't. To be honest, it surprised me. I thought he had it bad for me. I shook my head against the sudden tide of sadness. He obviously didn't have it bad enough.

I didn't know if we were on or off, but neither of us had called the other. I didn't know what to say. I felt as if I were adrift without him, but the thought of him questioning me every five seconds . . . not trusting me . . . no. I couldn't go through that again.

"What is it then?" Zeca started chopping again.

I tried forming my thoughts into words. I had never really wanted what Zeca had—until he got it. I'm not saying I wanted Antonio, but I wanted that closeness.

"It's the damn Bermuda triangle," I said. Now I was starting to feel depressed.

My brother laughed. "You mean Valentine's Day?"

"Yeah, Valentine's Day," I mimicked. For years we'd talked about Christmas, New Year's, and Valentine's Day as being an emotional Bermuda triangle, only my brother was now *a deux*. He and Antonio had spent Christmas in Sweden, New Year's in Milan with Antonio's family, and Zeca probably couldn't wait for Valentine's Day.

"I've never had a real Valentine before," he said as if reading my thoughts.

Damn him. I knew it was true. I wanted to hate him, but I couldn't. I was glad he was happy. I realized I wanted to feel the same sweeping passion as if I would die saying goodbye to my man, the way he always did with Antonio. I envied him and yet I feared that kind of connection. It was weird.

In some ways, Zeca and I were closer than ever. For instance, we'd started dressing alike. We often turned up to work wearing similar clothing. Dad thought it was great and encouraged us to dress alike. He thought it was good for business. We thought it was some weird coincidence, but it kept happening . . . like today. We were both dressed in jeans and blue T-shirts. Spooky.

There was also a new intimacy between us. I was able to talk to Zeca the way I couldn't talk to anybody else. We hadn't always been that way, in spite of being twins.

When I opened my mouth to speak, I found his gaze on my face.

"I don't feel shipwrecked without Hugh," I said. "Not the way you do with Antonio."

"Really? You've seemed so unhappy since he left. I'm worried about you, Alex."

Zeca's eyes conveyed compassion and understanding. I knew he felt a deep, abiding adoration for Antonio. What's more, I knew that super cop felt the same way about Zeca.

Our conversation was cut short by the trill of Italian opera. Zeca's face lit up. I knew it was Antonio calling him on his cell phone.

Hastily wiping his hands on a dishcloth, he shouldered the phone, cradling it to his ear. "*Il mio amore,*" he said. There was a long moment of silence, followed by an ear-splitting

6

grin. Whatever Antonio said sent my brother into fits of laughter.

Sickening. It was *sickening!*

I heard the sound of voices out front and peeked through the service window. Our first customers of the day were here. I picked up some menus and an order pad and stomped off to a table quickly filling with a group of travelers obviously new to the island. Their suitcases stood against the wall.

"Too bloody early to check in," one of the men griped. "Thought we'd stop off for breakfast."

Just my luck. Australians. They're cheap, and they're rude.

"I'm very glad you did," I said, issuing smiles and menus around the table.

It would be easy to calm the cranky Aussies once they had food and coffee in front of them. I called for Zeca, who came running. He was the only one who knew how to handle the new cappuccino machine. It really pissed me off. What was wrong with the old one, anyway? The new one made me feel stupid. Zeca made the coffees and ran off to cook omelets for our guests, leaving me to handle the new orders and table-clearing.

If only he didn't have to look so fucking happy about life.

The Australians complained about everything. The boat took too long getting here from Naples, the little funicular that brought them from the sea up the mountain to Capri Town was dinky. And of course, their villa wasn't ready yet.

They spread general ill will to other people around them who seemed to be having a wonderful time. They asked for more water when they'd barely taken a sip to begin with. They talked loudly enough for people to hear them clear across the other side of the island. And being Australian, it meant their tips would be utter crap.

We got a table full of British travelers. I suspected their tips wouldn't be much better and I tried not to react when they glopped ketchup on everything on their plates. My brother was an artist in the kitchen. I shook my head. Good food was wasted on some people.

I supposed I should feel guilty having that opinion since my family was British and Italian, but I didn't. I eavesdropped shamelessly on their conversation.

"Well, Jane said he's in here all the time, but it's kinda early. He's a TV actor. Maybe he's getting his beauty sleep," one of the women said. I knew they were talking about Dad. Toppy had been a big TV star in England but gave it all up to fulfill his long-cherished dream of opening a restaurant on Capri. He was in here every day when he wasn't busy making his girlfriend happy in the sack.

I had a horrible feeling he and Angie would get married and that meant I'd no longer have the house to myself. Toppy spent most nights with her, and Zeca was practically living with Antonio. I did *not* want to live with Dad and Angie. They were such a fight-and-fuck team. She was the local hotshot baker, and you could always tell when things were good between them because we got the choicest bread. When things were bad, we got . . . nothing.

"You wanted to meet Toppy?" I asked the British tourists, who were still whispering about him.

"Does he come in here?" one of the women asked.

"Yes, every day. He should be here by ten."

They hogged the table, sipping endless coffees while waiting for him. I wanted to swat them with our menus. The Australians wouldn't give up their table either and ordered more ice water. Yeah, they were the last of the big spenders.

Zeca and I went nonstop for a few hours, juggling tables, finding seats for new arrivals. Dad finally showed up, Antonio right behind him.

"Hi, Alex," Antonio said.

I put a hand on his shoulder as he blew past me. "How do you do that?"

Antonio stopped. "Do what?"

"How can you tell us apart? You always do that, even when Zeca and I dress alike."

He gave me a disarming smile. "You really want to know?"

"Yeah. I really want to know."

He leaned in, and I got a whiff of peppermint gum. He put his lips to my ear. "When I see your brother, my cock gets hard, and my heart beats faster."

"Shit."

He shrugged. "You asked."

I felt a weird gravitational pull and realized Zeca was in the room. He and Antonio stood, staring at one another. The sudden whoosh of heat between them was like opening an oven door. Without a word, they walked to the kitchen together.

"Has it been busy?" Toppy asked, his toothsome movie star grin on display. Dad loved the attention he got. He happily posed for photos with his fans, autographed their menus and travel guides, even their leftover boarding passes from their plane travel. I wondered how quickly these items would wind up on eBay.

Toppy Colombo was still a handsome man, with crinkly blue eyes and dark hair helped a little — well, a lot — by hair dye. He looked amazing for a guy in his fifties. Zeca and I had just turned twenty-six and had his more dominant genes. I glanced through the service window, noting Antonio and Zeca were nowhere to be seen. Man, their dicks would drop off at the rate they were doing it.

I scooped up empty dishes and coffee cups.

"Bring me a cafe latté, Zeca . . . I mean Alex," Toppy said

airily, waving his hand at me.

Bastard. He knows I can't work the damn machine. I was about to go and rain on my brother's romantic parade when he and Antonio clattered out of the stockroom, their faces shining. Antonio tucking his shirt into his pants, my brother buttoning up his Levi's fly. *Oh brother.*

"Dad wants a cappuccino," I said.

"You want one, too?" he asked Antonio, his fingers trailing across his lover's lips.

Antonio kissed them. "Yes," he said. "I live for your coffees."

Oh man . . . could he be any cornier?

They drifted into the restaurant as I dumped the dirty dishes in the kitchen sink. I saw Antonio taking a seat at a table for two. I noticed the possessive way he watched my brother working, oblivious to the looks on the faces of half the women in the restaurant. Antonio attracted a lot of attention. He was a big, macho guy. You'd never guess he was gay, except I knew he had big, macho feelings for my brother.

"You got any gay brothers or cousins?" I asked him, taking a seat beside him.

Antonio looked a bit startled. "Me?" He frowned. "I know a few guys . . . but none of your games would work on them, Alex."

"Games?" *Shit.*

He'd already lost interest in the conversation. He was back to staring at Zeca again.

One of the British women from the next table came over with a Capri street map. She batted her eyelids at Antonio and stuck her chest out at him.

I confess, I love men, but something about a big bosom enthralls me. I can't explain it. My father once said I enjoyed breastfeeding hugely when I was a baby. Our mother had abandoned us when Zeca and I were teenagers. Maybe I had a mother complex or something.

"Excuse me, officer," the woman said. "My friend and I," she pointed to a woman sitting at the table whose boobs were bursting out of her off-the-shoulder blouse, "we're visiting Capri, and we were wondering if you know where the Villa Potania is . . . we seem to have lost our way."

"Villa Potania?" Antonio took hold of the street map and pointed to a small side street off the Capri Town square. "It's just two blocks from here."

"Can you show us the way?"

"Yes. I'm showing you right here." His finger traced the line on the map.

Zeca arrived with cappuccinos for Dad, Antonio and even for me. That touched me. I had to admit, Zeca had a magical way with coffee.

"Sit awhile," he said to me. "You've been busy all morning."

Antonio gazed at my brother's crotch, then up at his face. "*Vi ringrazio, bell'uomo.*"

My brother smiled back. I sighed inwardly. *Thank you, beautiful man.* It was a lovely thing to say, and the emotion behind it almost unglued me. I brushed all thoughts of Hugh from my mind. Zeca seemed to find it hard to tear himself away as he went to greet two new arrivals. The woman with the street map stood beside us, looking uncertain for a moment.

"Can you show us the way?" she asked Antonio again.

A look of confusion crossed his face. "The way to where?"

Man, my brother must have blown the guy's brains out in the stockroom.

"I'll take you." Dad's voice boomed over their conversation. The woman looked dismayed but had no choice. She waited for Dad to finish his coffee. He was such a flirt. He kept up a running patter of jokes about the island, but the woman beside us kept staring at Antonio, who was busy flicking through cell phone messages.

"Gotta get back to work," he said. "The pickpockets have been busy this morning." He caught my brother's eye and winked at him before leaving, walking down the street with his coffee cup in hand. Only in Capri.

I wanted to chase after him. I wanted to promise I wouldn't play games with his friends, but I had the second-best thing to getting Antonio to work on my behalf. I had his other half. My brother . . . who was also *my* other half.

Cornering him in the kitchen, I put the idea to Zeca. I wanted my own macho Italian guy.

"Are you serious?" he asked as he sliced up some of Angie's freshly baked lemon and honey bread that he would use to make French toast. "No games?"

"What is it with you and Antonio?" Before he could respond, I assured him, "No games. Please, Zeca. I want to be in love. I want a great guy."

He looked up from his perfect slices and must have taken me at my word.

"All right," he said. "I'm on it."

I took a deep breath. I felt a huge weight lifting from my shoulders and from the pit of my stomach. I wanted a guy by Valentine's Day, but I could handle it being a bit later than that. I'd just spend the day in bed with the covers over my head until it was over.

I realized nobody was waiting on tables since Toppy was still attempting to charm the two female tourists, and I ran into the restaurant—just in time to see a guy crouched behind the counter, trying to break into the cash register.

Chapter Two

A ntonio made a swift, brief reappearance, arresting the guy. The thief wasn't difficult to find. Toppy had hard-tackled the guy and was sitting on him by the time Antonio arrived with his handcuffs. Antonio got a round of applause from the tourists, a second cup of coffee and private, sexy, meaningful glances from my brother for his policing efforts.

My brother got a ton of private, sexy, meaningful glances from Antonio.

Toppy got pats on the back and a lot more requests for autographs.

I got, as I predicted, a lousy tip from the Australian tourists.

Toppy went off with the two women to show them the way to their villa. They were a lot happier to be escorted by him now that they thought he was some kind of hero.

Thirty minutes later I began to wonder if he'd lost his way back but soon became too involved with early lunch traffic to clock-watch any longer.

"We have weevils," my brother said in a dramatic tone, sidling up beside me. "I just opened the bean and barley mix we got from London yesterday. It's crawling with weevils."

"Ewww."

"Exactly. So, the bean soup's off. We've got all the others. Peddle the *zuppa*."

"Right. What's in it again?"

He looked at me. I could never remember ingredients to anything except a cup of coffee.

"Kale, leeks, red peppers, sweet Italian sausage, and a dash of cream. Push it as much as you can. We've got loads of it."

"Any other soups?"

"Yes, the Basilicata fish soup is made with cod, garlic, and olive oil. We're serving it with matera bread."

"Matera bread." I paused. "That's supposed to be the best bread in Italy."

He smiled then. "Yes, it is."

I knew that matera originated in Naples, the closest big city to the island. According to Antonio, who grew up in Naples, Angie's version of the bread was as good as anything you could get in the city.

I couldn't believe how many people wanted the damn bean soup—and the irritable way they greeted the news that it wasn't available. Zeca was much better dealing with the fussy patrons. He never once raised his voice and never looked like he wanted to punch them out. By the time he finished bullshitting, he somehow managed to convince them that leek and potato soup was their own idea.

He turned on his heel and galloped off to the kitchen to garnish his soup bowls. I started to panic as the doors filled with hungry patrons. We were packed to the rafters.

Where the hell was Toppy?

In the kitchen, my brother's sexual euphoria finally broke long enough for him to have a mild meltdown. He's got this weird thing about running out of teaspoons. A phobia, you might say. I'll admit I used to hide them just to torture him, but lately, I've been too busy being depressed to screw around with flatware. These days the teaspoons seem to be vanishing on their own.

"Where's Dad?" Zeca asked as he ran back and forth between the cappuccino machine and the sink. He snapped on yellow gloves and began to frantically wash dishes by hand.

I did feel a pang of guilt that I'd left the dirty dishes in the sink, so I grabbed a tea towel and dried off a few things as he handed them to me.

"He walked the titty ladies to their villa . . . er, I mean the British ladies."

"That was an hour ago." My brother eyed the clock. There was a knock at the kitchen door.

"Oh crap!" he hissed. "Trouble!"

"Don't open it," I begged him.

"Are you crazy? I *have* to open it. We need the bread. We mowed through every last crust this morning." He took off his gloves and walked to the door. You might say he had a right to be nervous. Hell hath no fury like an Italian woman scorned. You can take my word on that.

"Angie," he said. Personally, I think he did a tremendous job of acting calm and friendly, warm, inviting even, but Angie wasn't fooled. She could smell desperation on a man like other people can smell body odor. Or another woman's perfume.

"Where is he?"

"Er . . ."

She pushed past Zeca, dumping a huge basket of fresh bread on the sideboard. She peered through the service window into the packed restaurant.

"Where is he?" she asked again, hands on hips.

Oh no. She was in what Toppy calls her mad cow stance. Any second now she'd launch into a full-scale attack.

Toppy entered the kitchen at that moment. I would have breathed a sigh of relief . . . if his face hadn't been covered in red lipstick, and his shirt wasn't buttoned up haphazardly. His hair stuck out in odd spikes.

My brother's hands moved to his face. I backed away, hoping to save the bread she'd just brought.

"Hello?" one of the patrons called out.

Disaster!

Angie took it all in, and Toppy began to shake in his shoes.

"No!" my brother shouted as she lunged for a thick breadstick from her basket then whacked my father in the head.

Zeca snatched the bread from her hands. He tossed it to me before thrusting the basket into my arms. "Hide it!" he shouted.

I ran next door to the chocolate shop and hid it behind the counter, where the shopkeeper was busy munching her own inventory. She was reading a dog-eared paperback copy of *Water for Elephants*.

How apt.

She raised a brow. "She's smacking him again?" she asked around a mouthful of caramels.

I nodded and ran from the store, back into the restaurant. My brother was rushed off his feet putting food in front of patrons as if the pantomime in the kitchen wasn't taking place.

Toppy was busy trying to placate Angie, who chased him into the restaurant.

"Where. Is. The. Bread?" she asked Zeca in menacing tones. She never could tell us apart.

When he couldn't give her a satisfactory response, she hauled back and kneed him in the balls.

Every man in the restaurant felt it. You could hear the collective, "Ooooh!"

My brother dropped to his knees, tears in his eyes. Antonio wouldn't appreciate Angie breaking his favorite toys. I felt a tremor of pleasure . . . then felt instantly guilty. Zeca's mouth hung open, tears of pain streaking down his face.

Toppy ran back to the kitchen and returned with a bag of frozen peas, handing them to my brother. All our patrons stared as Zeca toppled to the side, moaning and groaning. I knelt beside him and grabbed the peas, shoving them onto his crotch.

Zeca stopped making any sounds at all. It was scary.

"Breathe," I commanded, rubbing his arm.

"What happened?"

I looked up to see Antonio standing over us, a murderous expression on his face. Toppy dragged Angie out of the restaurant.

Antonio dropped to the floor beside my brother, cradling his head. He glared at me. "Did you hurt him?"

I shook my head. "Of course not."

"Angie," Zeca whispered.

"Angie?" Antonio's cheek muscle twitched. I knew he wouldn't go after her and slug her.

"She thought I was Alex," my brother mumbled.

Antonio's eyes narrowed, and I was very glad the cops in Capri didn't carry guns. He helped Zeca into the kitchen. It was quite pathetic watching him limp. I bit my lip. I had no idea what the hell to do with the food and people were getting antsy.

"Is it extra for the floor show?" somebody asked. I was about to snap off a bitter retort, but he was a cute guy, and my gaydar shifted to code red.

"It's built into your entertainment tax," I quipped and rushed off to the kitchen. Antonio and Zeca were piling food onto plates. My poor brother looked like he was in agony, but he kept working, Antonio standing close beside him.

"Take these out." Antonio pointed to three plates. "Table five." He nuzzled my brother. "What do I put on this plate, *bello*?"

I would have objected to taking orders from him, but things were so crazy, and his manner was so calm, it helped ground me.

Back and forth I went, Antonio and Zeca assembling perfect dishes in the kitchen. We got the food out in record time, and then Toppy came back.

"Is Zeca okay?" he asked me.

"He's in a lot of pain."

"I'm sorry. Those women threw themselves at me."

"Nooo . . . I don't want to hear it."

My big concern was not having bread anymore. I really didn't give a toss about my father's love life. He manhandled the cappuccino machine, which made some gruesome sounds. To cover up his ineptitude, I started giving people free limoncello liqueurs. One small glass of Toppy's homemade concoction could tame a wild elephant. Half the restaurant was drunk by the time we finished serving the meals and started producing dessert dishes.

Antonio came out with Zeca's homemade lemon sorbet in half-lemon shells. It had become our new specialty. Antonio was great with the patrons, and my brother did an odd little hobble out to the cappuccino machine, sending my father into the kitchen to handle the remaining food orders.

"*Bello*, three cappuccinos and a macchiato for table four," Antonio said.

The three of us worked as a team, Antonio and I racing around with coffees and hot chocolates, but I sensed his anger toward me. I kept going to the chocolate shop to retrieve loaves of bread. We now had none left for the evening shift, and I knew Angie wouldn't be bringing us any more.

"We'll make some," Toppy, the eternal optimist, said when we closed for afternoon siesta. It was a firm rule on the island. Everyone closed for three hours and then re-opened, staying open late into the evening.

"Who's *we*?" my brother asked, still clutching frozen foods against his injured nether region.

"Not you, *bello*," Antonio said. "I'm taking you home to rest."

He put his arm around Zeca and steered him out of the restaurant.

Toppy and I stared after them for a moment.

"What do you know about baking bread?" Dad asked me at last.

"Fuck all. You?"

"About the same." He stuck out his bottom lip. "I've managed to convince Angelina that nothing happened with those two women. I said it was just kisses, but it might . . . you know . . . take a day or two for her to calm down."

"Is that the truth? That nothing happened?"

He had the grace to blush. "Yes and no."

"I don't think I want to hear this."

"To tell you the truth, the spirit was willing, but the flesh was . . . not so much."

"You couldn't get it up?"

"Do you have to shout it across the bloody island?"

"Is it like that with Angie?"

He shook his head, looking shocked. "I think she's done some voodoo or something on me, mate. Look, can't you talk to her? Can't you convince her I'm blameless and that I love her?"

"Do we need bread that badly?"

Toppy looked at me. We both knew the answer to that question. Zeca could bake a few loaves but the evening shift would be horrendous, even with our part-time waiters who came in to help each night. Zeca wouldn't have time to produce endless loaves and Toppy, and I were worse than useless when it came to doing more than taking orders, plating and bringing out dishes.

I was pretty good at buttering bread, not making it.

"She likes you," he said.

"That's why she attacked me today . . . or who she thought was me?"

He spread out his hands. "She's a little emotional."

"A little? Dad, she's nuts."

"She will cripple our business. And speaking of nuts, she's hobbled your brother. It'll be worse for us unless we grovel."

"Oh, all right." I wasn't happy. I downed a limoncello and stomped out of the café, leaving Toppy to lock up. He would give me enough time to talk to Angelina before coming home.

I climbed the eighty-eight stone stairs from the piazza up to our street. In truth, I had no idea how Toppy managed to have so much sex after negotiating those stairs every day. Horniness must run in our family though, because my father, brother, and I thought about sex pretty much nonstop.

At the top of the stairs, I took a deep breath. Angie was baking. I could smell the bread from where I stood. I couldn't tell if this was a good or bad sign since she baked no matter what her mood. I walked around the back of our house to her home. Toppy always came and went this way, as if he believed nobody knew they were seeing each other.

I took another fortifying breath, hesitating before knocking at her door.

"It worked. I tell you it worked!" I heard her saying. She was speaking in rapid-fire Italian, but I was fluent in the language and understood every word. I stopped seconds before my knuckles could touch the heavy wooden door.

"Yes! Yes! I did exactly what you told me to do! I file my fingernails into Toppy's coffee every morning. He's mine. *Mine!*"

Was she joking? I heard her mad laughter, my eyes rolling around in my head. What did she mean by those words? She was pacing her kitchen now. I could hear her high heels clacking against the ancient linoleum.

"I'm telling you, he has no clue. I've done everything you

20

said. I buried the bottle full of rusty nails in his back garden. Do you know how hard it was to find so many rusty nails? I spat in his cocktail last night. I spit in it every night. So the first and last thing he tastes every day is me! He told me the soup with the herbs you sent me tasted funny. I didn't make it again. Other than that, I've done everything you said, and it worked, but he tried fooling around on me today, and he couldn't do it! He has no idea I have complete control over — What's that? Oh . . . okay. I'll wait."

She moved over to the oven. I could hear her banging the door. I took the opportunity to glance in her window. She was naked except for her high heels. Her butt and the rest of her body were amazingly tight for a woman who was all about bread. She held her phone against her ear, straightening again.

"Madame Zelda . . . can I make him marry me?" she asked. "I mean, what can I do to convince him?"

I ducked out of sight, creeping along the vine-covered trellis that stretched from her back gate to ours. I crept through our back door and locked it behind me. Toppy stood there hovering in the kitchen, waiting for me.

"Well?" he asked, his eyes darting back and forth. I'd never seen him so anxious.

"Sit down. I have something to tell you."

"Oh, and I've got something to tell *you*. Some guy came to the café looking for you. He said you waited on him at lunchtime."

"Really?"

"Yeah. He said he'd come back tonight."

That inspired me. I hoped it was the cute guy I'd noticed but got too busy to talk to.

"He said his name is Stefano."

"Stefano!" I rocked on my heels. I liked the name already. I could have drifted away into a mental sea of happiness, but

I had to tell my father that his girlfriend was demented.

"Sit down," I said again.

"I don't want to sit down."

"You'll want to when you hear what I have to tell you."

"Just tell me," he said, sounding exasperated.

"She files her fingernails into your coffee every morning. She buried a jar of rusty nails in the garden." I pointed a shaky finger at him. "She put weird herbs in your soup and . . . she spits in your drinks."

"*What?*" He gagged, grabbing his throat. "She poisoned me!"

"Dad . . . you've got to calm yourself."

"I gotta sit down," he said, looking absolutely petrified. "You really think she buried a jar of nails in the garden?"

"We can always check later tonight."

"I'm not digging up the whole bloody garden!"

"What are you going to do?"

He threw himself into a chair in the living room, running a hand over his face. "God, I don't know."

We were interrupted by a knock at the door. We both jumped.

"Toppy?"

My father's left eye twitched as he gripped me for support. "Oh God, it's her."

"Stay calm," I said. "If we're very quiet, maybe she'll think nobody's home."

Dad trembled. "That won't stop her. She's not just barmy, mate. She's absolutely sodding crackers!"

Angie knocked again, and we shook like jellies, staring at the door. She turned the handle and poked her head around the door. My father's fingers dug into my arms in an uncomfortable way. His mouth hung open in a strange parody of the Toppy Colombo toothy grin.

"You gave her a key?" I hissed.

"Toppy?" she asked, her whole body appearing in the kitchen. She'd thrown on a dress and was still wearing her high heels. "Did I hear you say crackers?" She advanced toward us.

My father made a strange gurgling sound low in his throat.

"Crackers?" I tried to play it off. "No."

"You're not thinking of replacing my bread with cheap crackers, are you, Toppy?"

He shook his head. His mouth had apparently forgotten how to work.

"I'm sure I heard you mention crackers," she said. "Just when I was going to forgive you."

"You misunderstood," I said. She glanced from my face to my crotch. I had a horrible feeling she was thinking about shoving her knee into it, and I tried angling my body away from her. "We were talking about weevils."

"Huh?" Toppy looked bewildered.

"I was just saying that Zeca found weevils in the barley and bean mix . . . remember?"

"Snarflefordlrr . . ." Toppy said. At least, that's what it sounded like. I'd never seen my father so terrified of anything. Even the network's constant threats of axing his TV soap opera hadn't affected him this way. On the other hand, maybe the strain did get to him, which was why he moved here in the first place.

"Where did you get the barley and beans?" Angie asked. She sure was in an inquisitive mood. She reminded me of Hugh and his endless questions.

"Toppy imported it from London."

"Come and have a drink." She plunked her hand between us and grabbed my father's arm.

"I can't," he said, his mouth in sudden working order.

"Just one." She had a weird smile on her face and gave

him a little wiggle of her ass. "We have a sexy little drink, and then you can go to work."

"No, no. I can't. Alex and I are leaving town tomorrow."

"We are?" I almost screamed when his fingernails dug into the flesh on my arm.

"I told you, we have to leave first thing in the morning, so no late night for you." He lifted his hand from me, wagging his finger. "First thing. Very, very early."

"But I don't understand. Where are you going? Am I invited?"

"No, sorry," Toppy said. "We have urgent family business."

"Where?" Angie looked really pissed.

"St. Tropez."

"St. Tropez?"

Why did that suddenly seem familiar? I hunted through my memory banks.

"You're going to the south of France?"

"His boyfriend." Toppy's thumb jerked toward me. "His family has bought a little café in St. Tropez, and they want our business advice."

She looked about as stunned as I felt. "I can understand you taking Zeca . . . but Alex?"

"Geez, thanks a lot," I said.

"I can leave Zeca to run the restaurant here . . . but Alex works pretty hard. Alex is . . . well, like I said, it's his boyfriend's café."

She stood silently fuming. Her mad cow stance looked like it was going to turn into full-scale-rabid mode. I half expected her head to swivel around on its axis and pea soup to come hurling out of her mouth. "You can't go. I won't allow it," she said.

"You won't—" Toppy laughed then. "You can't be serious. This is an excellent business opportunity, and I want to see both my sons settled. Zeca has a wonderful man in his life, and I want to see Alex happy with Hugh."

Hugh . . . oh my God. He was in the south of France. When the hell had Dad been in touch with him? If Toppy wasn't BSing Angie then I would be seeing Hugh the following day!

"You're not going," she said.

"Oh yes, I am."

She swallowed hard. Her anger dissolved and she began to cry.

Oh, what a performance!

"I'll be back," he said, standing and reaching over, patting her shoulder.

"When?" She almost shouted the word.

"A week . . . two at the most."

Angie threw herself into his arms, and my dad comforted her for a full thirty seconds.

"We have to go," he said. "I'll talk to you when I get back tonight."

"But it's siesta time."

"Siesta? We had the busiest day today, and tomorrow Alex and I are leaving. We have to meet and talk to Zeca . . . tonight we won't get the chance."

"You'll come to me tonight after you close the restaurant?"

"Of course," he said. He kissed her and I could tell it was his movie star kiss, not his lover's kiss. The bloom was definitely off this rose.

We shuffled outside, my dad dragging me down the street. At the top of the stairs leading down to the piazza, he let out a breath.

"Piece of cake," he said. "Now comes the tricky part." He hauled me down the stairs with him.

"That didn't look like a piece of cake!" I yelled, trying hard to keep up with him.

"Yeah, it was. The hard part will be convincing your brother."

At the bottom of the stairs we turned left, and I felt guilty as we ran down the street to Antonio's mountainside cottage. I could see whiffs of smoke coming from the chimney, and I imagined they were making love by the fireplace.

I was worried about crashing their solitude, but to my surprise, they didn't answer the door.

"They're in there," Dad said. "I hear them kissing."

He kept pounding on the door, and Antonio eventually answered, a sullen look on his face. He had a blanket wrapped around his waist. I looked past him to my brother, clearly naked under a giant piece of lambskin on the floor in front of a roaring fire.

A minute later and I think we might have caught them actually having sex.

"What are you doing here?" Zeca asked, sitting up. He didn't look pleased, and neither did Antonio.

Dad leaped into the room, and I followed. Antonio closed the door. Dad explained his problem.

"You're going to St. Tropez tomorrow to hide from your girlfriend?" Zeca asked.

"Yes. We'll be gone, like I said, a week, two at the most."

"Give us a moment." Antonio held his hand down to my brother and helped him up. They scuttled off to what I assumed was the bedroom.

They had left a bottle of red wine and two half-filled glasses on the floor.

Dad lunged for them, passing me one.

"Waste not, want not," he said, downing the contents of his glass. I took a sip of mine. Very smooth. I was certain it was expensive.

I took a quick look around. The cottage was furnished in a masculine way but very warm. There was a sofa, two wing chairs, and a coffee table that all looked like they'd been pushed back to accommodate their fireplace friskiness. I noticed a couple of photos of them together in frames. My heart pined to feel that happy and in love.

I heard their voices in the bedroom but couldn't hear what they were saying.

Zeca and Antonio returned, fully dressed. Antonio brought out two more glasses from the kitchen and poured more wine for us all. "Please. Sit down."

My father and I took the wing chairs, Antonio sitting close to my brother on the sofa. His arm moved around Zeca.

They exchanged a long look. It seemed to speak volumes, then Antonio looked across the small expanse of space at us. Zeca let him do all the talking.

"As it happens, maybe this could be a good thing. My mother owned a restaurant in Naples. She had to give it up when I refused to let her pay the Camorra the protection money they wanted."

"Yes, yes, I remember," Toppy said. "That's how you got demoted and sent here."

Antonio nodded. "She's a wonderful cook. She's in Milan now, as you know, but she really misses cooking, she misses her restaurant and . . . I'm sure she would come and help Zeca." He smiled at my brother, who buried his face in Antonio's neck.

"My mother already loves Zeca. I think they would work well together. I'll be here. I can help out sometimes, and you have your part-time staff. Maybe we can get them to work a few extra hours. We'll be fine."

"Excellent!" Toppy said, slapping his hands together. "This is better than I thought."

"My mother bakes bread," Antonio said. "She knows Angie well . . . I am sure they can come to an understanding."

"Really? An understanding. How wonderful." Toppy

stood and bounced on his toes. I hadn't seen him so happy since he won a BAFTA award.

"An understanding," he said again as if he didn't understand what that meant. I hoped bread wars weren't going to be in the immediate future for Café Toppy.

"And now, if you don't mind, Zeca and I have some unfinished business of our own," Antonio said.

"Right, right . . . oh . . . yes. Well . . . we'll see you at the restaurant." Toppy sculled his wine and plucked at my T-shirt sleeve. We scooted away from the house again, hurrying along the road back to the restaurant.

"We'd better book a flight," Toppy said. "Geez. I better call Hugh's dad. You know, your brother found himself a great guy. I'll marry *you* off, then . . ."

"Then what?"

"I don't know," he said. "I hope by the time I come back Angie forgets all about me."

"Yeah, right."

He closed his eyes and stopped moving for a second. "I'll think twice before I dip my wick again, son. You can take me at my word."

"Yeah, right," I said again.

We hurried into the restaurant. In the tiny back office, we had a desktop computer. We could book our trip from there.

"When did they call you?" I asked. "Why didn't Hugh call me himself?"

"Because you're both stubborn," Toppy said. "His father says Hugh is depressed. He misses you."

"He misses me?"

"You got sand in your ears?" Toppy asked. "Yeah. He misses you."

I glanced out the window. I watched snuggling couples pass us by on their early *passeggiata,* evening stroll. I wanted that. I wanted that intimacy.

"Dad," I said. "Are we really going to St. Tropez?"

"Yeah." He playfully punched my arm. "Son of a gun. We're going on a holiday!"

CHAPTER THREE

Toppy spent all evening holed up in his miniscule office, demanding endless cups of coffee and several helpings of Zeca's new dessert, lemon cream cake he'd baked from Antonio's mother's recipe. Antonio arrived around nine o'clock when the restaurant was hopping. He looked moon-faced when Zeca offered him a slice.

"It's better than even the way my mother makes it," Antonio said. He gave Zeca a swift glance. "Don't ever tell her I said that."

He took over the cappuccino machine. I was a little put out that he and Zeca seemed to have mastered the peculiar beast, but it made things run a lot smoother in the restaurant. Zeca was now free to whip up more of his cakes since the demand was high. News about Zeca's cake had traveled fast. Late diners showed up for cake and coffee, and my poor brother was still icing freshly baked cakes at eleven o'clock that night. Not that he seemed to mind. I could see that between him and Antonio, we'd be leaving the joint in very capable hands.

"Did I hear Antonio's voice?" Dad asked, rushing out of the office. Normally he preened around the restaurant, but tonight he'd hunkered over his computer like he was working on some top-secret mission. He dragged Antonio away from the cappuccino machine.

"I can do this," one of our nighttime waiters muttered, eyeing the coffeemaker. "I'm not afraid of the machine." His left eye twitched, and his hand shook, belying his brave words.

Zeca asked me to take slices of cake and cappuccinos to Dad and Antonio, who huddled over maps and flight schedules. They thanked me and bent their heads back over their work again. By the time I came out, the cappuccino machine was back in Zeca's custody and, he informed me Stefano, the cutie who said he'd come to look for me, had been and gone.

"What? Already? Man, I was hoping for a hot date," I griped.

I watched my brother run a knife over the top of his massive cake, smoothing out the lemon icing with one hand as he held a jug of milk under the frothing tool on the cappuccino machine with the other.

"You have a hot date with Hugh tomorrow, remember?"

I shrugged. "Yeah, I guess."

He poured milk and foam into an assembled array of coffees and began slicing the cake as the waiters took care of the hot drinks.

"Here." Zeca gave me a piece of his cream cake as a sort of consolation prize. It was as fantastic as everyone said it was. The cake was lighter than air, the cream filling lemony and moist.

"This is amazing." I shoveled it down my throat so fast, my brother beamed when I licked the plate clean.

"Thank you. It's fun to make. Want another piece?"

"Hell no." I would be thankful to spend time away from my brother. If I hung out here any longer, I'd eat up everything he ever made, and I'd have to buy big-boy pants. I didn't think Hugh would dig a tubby boyfriend.

"Have you called him?" Zeca asked as I caved and hoed into my second slice of cake.

"Nuh-uh."

"Don't you think you should?"

"No. He can call me, too, you know."

"You were such an ass to him," Zeca insisted. "You really should make the first move."

"I wasn't an ass."

"Oh yeah, you were."

I would have argued the point but Stefano, the cute guy, was back. I rushed out to greet him as he paused in the doorway. He looked uncertain for a second until he saw me, and his face lit up. We traded grins, and I was suddenly sad to be leaving the next day.

"Alex."

I turned and found my brother beckoning me.

In the kitchen, he put his hands on my shoulders. "Don't do it."

"What?" But I knew. He was telling me not to screw things up. I gazed longingly out at Stefano, who took a seat at a small table with only one chair. I knew my brother was right, but I couldn't help myself. I rushed right back out to the guy's table. *Damn! He's so hot!*

"Hey," Stefano said, or at least, I assumed it was Stefano. He reached over and took my hand. "You're a hard guy to get hold of."

"Not really," I assured him. I brought him cake and coffee on the house and ignored my brother's steely stare.

For the rest of the evening, Stefano and I talked in sound bites. A sentence here, a word there. I gleaned he was staying at the ultra-luxurious villa, the I Faraglioni, which was about the most expensive place on the island. It rented, in low season, for the bargain price of fourteen thousand U.S. dollars a week. I wondered if he was very rich and how long he'd be here.

Dammit. Why did I let Toppy talk me into going away? *Hugh,* I reminded myself. *Unfinished business.*

The lure of Stefano and unblemished *new* business pulled

at me with brute force. I would just tell Toppy I wasn't going to St. Tropez.

Around midnight, he zoomed out of his office and waved maps and printouts around.

"We fly out first thing," he said and rushed away again.

As we prepared to close for the night, Stefano lingered. "Your brother hates me," he said at one point.

"No, he doesn't."

Dad raced out of his office just as I'd managed to persuade Stefano to wait outside for me. He brandished a ton of paperwork.

"Who's that? What are you doing?" Dad's nose twitched. "You don't have a date, do you? We're all set. We leave first thing in the morning. I debated going by boat since it's about four hundred and fifty miles away, but that would take a few days, even though I have friends heading that way. So we'll fly from Naples to Paris, and we'll drive down the coast. It'll take us about eight hours from Paris."

"Okay," I said, my spirits spiraling to my feet. I could hear Antonio and Zeca talking in the kitchen. I turned and caught their gazes. I didn't want a lecture about my relationship with Hugh . . . or with Stefano.

"We're leaving at six o'clock in the morning, Alex."

"I'll be there." I gave Toppy a wave and took off.

"You have to pack!" he shouted, but my attention was already on Stefano, who gave me a lazy grin as he waited for me under a streetlight.

"Where to?" he asked.

"Alex."

I turned and saw my brother beckoning me. "Later," I said.

"No. Now."

"Later." I turned away from him, leading Stefano down the street.

"He's a bossy brother," Stefano said.

"Yeah. Tell me about it." My cell phone rang, and I ignored it. "You feel like a drink?" I asked Stefano.

"Sure. The piazza is still hopping." He seemed nervous all of a sudden, which I found endearing.

In the little square on Via Camerelle, we found an outdoor table at a corner bar. The place was hopping like he said. We sat down, the waiter proffering a bottle of limoncello. Man, I felt like I was cheating on Hugh, drinking it with another guy. Heck, I *was* cheating on Hugh. Period.

"No. You have any nocino?" I asked, my voice coming out harsher than I'd intended.

"Of course." The waiter looked affronted.

"I'll have that, too," Stefano said of the walnut liqueur that was another island favorite. I adored it. I was surprised Stefano liked it, but so far, I liked everything about the guy.

My cell phone rang again. What the heck was going on?

I pulled it out and checked the readout as Stefano stood, waving at somebody.

"There's Pasquale," he said.

Who the hell was Pasquale? I scrolled through a message from my brother.

Call me. Urgent.

I glanced up as a tall, gangly, sandy-haired Frenchman joined us.

"Alex . . . this is my husband, Pasquale, and we were wondering if you'd be interested in joining us at the villa. He noticed you a couple of days ago and, well, we'd love it."

"A threesome?"

They nodded.

The drinks arrived, and I closed my eyes. I'd often fantasized about threesomes — but it was the last thing I wanted.

God's punishing me for not calling Hugh.

"Sorry," I said. I left the nocino on the server's tray and walked away from the piazza.

Damn. I couldn't believe it. I hurried home, wondering what I would say if I called Hugh . . . or even if I *should* call. I started climbing the stairs to our house and stopped. No time like the present. I got Hugh's voicemail. I left a message, letting him know we'd be there tomorrow.

Back home, the house was empty. I thought Toppy must have been next door at Angelina's, or he wasn't home yet. I threw some clothes and a couple of books into a small suitcase and packed my laptop in its computer bag. Then I lay on my bed, my mind racing. Hugh was more attached to his cell phone than I was. It was weird he hadn't called back. I got out of bed, restless. I went downstairs then called a second and a third time, and even a fourth. I left two voicemail messages and a text.

Holy moly, he was ignoring me. What if he didn't want to see me? Then I'd be stuck!

I could hear impassioned sounds coming from Angelina's. I rolled my eyes. Dad was getting, er . . . lucky. Unbelievable. In spite of all the creepy things she'd been doing, he couldn't help himself. He still had to get his love. I sure wished I could call my brother, but I knew he was probably busy getting lucky, too.

Two seconds later, my cell phone rang. It was Zeca.

"What's wrong?" he asked. "I can feel you. Why didn't you call me?"

"Hugh isn't returning my calls."

"Where are you?"

"I'm home."

A long pause. "Give him a chance, Alex. He'll call you."

"No, he won't, and I'm gonna look like an ass showing up in St. Tropez tomorrow."

Another pause. I could hear him talking to Antonio.

"We're on our way."

I took a big breath and waited. I thanked whatever lucky

stars I had that my brother had tuned into me and called. I found myself being more upset than I had been in a long time. For the first time in two weeks, I allowed myself to think back to the night Hugh, and I had fought, and he'd left the island.

We'd had a wonderful start to our evening. It had been my evening off. We spent the whole afternoon in bed. I swallowed over the lump forming in my throat. I'd taken for granted that he was staying with me. We got along so well. Our sex life was giddy, our kisses endless. I had never met a man who enjoyed kissing as much as I did.

He surprised me with dinner at Da Paolino, a wonderful, romantic restaurant in the middle of a lemon grove, and . . . and . . .

He asked me to marry him.

I went berserk.

In hindsight, I probably *was* an ass, but marriage was a huge leap for me, and he wanted an answer immediately. I thought that was unreasonable. Now I wondered why I'd been so panic-stricken. I remembered Hugh becoming hysterical. He'd had no idea I would react the way I did and frankly, neither did I.

I'd run off through a field of lemon trees. Now, when I smelled the strong scent of wild lemons, I thought back to that night. Oh, if I could do it all again!

I heard a noise outside the back door. I knew my brother wouldn't be entering the house that way, so I peered out the kitchen window. My dad was in his jeans and no top, skulking around our backyard. I opened the door. He had a flashlight in his hands and pointed the beam at me.

"What are you doing, Dad?"

"Shhh." He looked a mess and was tiptoeing around. He glanced back at me then trotted over.

"Look. I can't believe she said the things she did . . . that she buried a jar of nails."

I was indignant. "Are you saying I made those things up?"

"No, no. I'm thinking you misunderstood."

"I *didn't* misunderstand."

"She's so hot in the sheets I can't give her up, son! I don't want to go away tomorrow . . . on the other hand, my track record for headcases is legendary."

His gaze swung away from me to the back garden.

A noise from inside the house alerted me to my brother's arrival. I turned to see Zeca and Antonio striding toward me.

"What's going on?" Antonio asked, looking over my shoulder at Dad.

"Oh great!" Toppy hissed. "I try to dig up the garden in secret, and you three turn it into a friggin' pajama party!"

"Is he looking for that jar of nails?" Zeca asked.

I nodded.

"Relax," Antonio said. "I'll help Toppy look while you and Alex have a little talk."

Zeca and I made fresh coffee. I knew I wouldn't get any sleep that night and once Dad found those rusty nails, he wouldn't want any shut-eye either. For two guys trying to be quiet they made a bit of noise out there, but so far Angie hadn't swooped in on them.

"You okay?" Zeca asked.

"I'm fine."

We stood in the kitchen, staring at each other.

"When did we become so fearful?" he asked me. "I remember us being the most tenacious, reckless guys I knew."

"We grew up," I said, toeing a crack in the kitchen linoleum.

"Nah. It was more than that."

"It was her, wasn't it?" My gut twisted in pain.

"Yeah." Zeca's voice was quiet. He looked out the window. I could see dirt flying out there. "Mum fucked us up royally."

We watched Dad and Antonio crouching over a spot in the garden.

"Yeah, I guess she did." I sighed. "I screwed up saying no to Hugh's proposal."

"No, you didn't."

He surprised me. My brother was such a romantic.

"Alex, you screwed up not explaining why you weren't ready. You hurt his feelings and made him feel stupid. He deserved better than that." He put his hand on my shoulder. "Dad gave me a piece of advice I'm going to give you."

"Save it. Dad's advice has to be totally barmy."

"No, it's not." Zeca shook his head. "I listened to him. It didn't make sense at first, but it's true, and it works. He said, 'You have to love before you can be relentless.'"

I stared at him. "Like I said, barmy."

"No, it's not. Alex, that advice allowed me to feel . . . safe enough to love. It—"

"Oh, Zeec. It's easy for *you* to say. You're living on the most beautiful island in the world with a hot guy who's crazy about you—"

"Hey," he said. "I had a complete meltdown the day I went to Naples with Antonio. And you know what? I was forced to see everything . . . to deal with all the shit I'd forgotten was buried so deep. I fell in love with Antonio, but there were no guarantees. No safety net. No rehearsals. There aren't for any of us."

"He loves you."

Zeca stared at me, and all his ghosts lingered in his eyes. "And I love him. There were days after I got back from Naples that I thought I would die. I thought I wouldn't be able to live if he didn't want me."

God, that made me feel awful. I was the one who'd kept them apart.

"I'm sorry, Zeec."

He smiled then. "Don't be. Antonio was . . . relentless. He came here with a ladder and climbed to my room one night. It was the most amazing night of my life. I got what Dad was talking about. Antonio brings out the best in me. I like to think I do the same for him."

"A ladder, huh?"

He nodded. "And I learned how to be relentless, too."

There was a cry from the garden. We stopped talking.

Dad came in, tears streaking down his face. He held up a shaky hand. In it was a huge, dirty jar—filled with rusty nails.

"She frickin' did it, man. I can't believe it!" He threw himself into Zeca's arms.

"Can you go help Antonio fill in the dirt?" my brother asked as Dad fell apart. I went straight outside. I found Antonio covered in mud, trying to fill in all the spaces.

"Thanks." He smiled at me.

"Thank you for loving my brother," I whispered back.

Antonio's grin was huge as we worked in silence. We found a bone and looked at each other. I didn't even want to know if it was animal or human.

A light came on in Angelina's kitchen.

"Hurry!" Antonio glanced at her window as we filled the last hole and fled to our kitchen. We bolted the door behind us, turning off the lights.

Angie bellowed for my dad. We heard her back door open.

We all breathed heavily.

She came out of her house, still yelling for him, banged her back door closed again and then everything went quiet.

"I guess I'm going to St. Tropez," Dad said.

"It isn't the Gulag," Zeca responded, which made all of us laugh.

The house phone rang.

"That'll be her. I'll tell her I couldn't sleep and came home to pack." Dad walked toward the phone like a man going to the plank.

"Who wants cake?" my brother asked, switching on the light. We washed our hands before handling the food. Now that I looked around the room, the only one clean was my brother.

The four of us had cake and coffee, and I found new respect for Antonio for helping Dad dig up the garden.

We kept talking about the problem of Angie and what Dad was going to do.

"I can't make any decisions. I need to think," he said. He let Antonio take charge of the jar, which he said he would dispose of.

"I don't believe in spells," Antonio said, "but this is the creepiest thing I ever saw."

We talked until the sun rose, Zeca whipping up eggs and hot buttered bread. I didn't want to leave the sanctity of the island, but when I saw the way Antonio hugged and kissed Zeca, I knew.

I had to grab my own ladder, such as it was, and go off in search of Hugh.

Dad and I showered and changed. We grabbed our bags and Zeca, and Antonio walked down to the funicular with us. I hugged my brother and didn't want to let go. I'd had a long few hours to think about what he'd said.

"I'm just a phone call away," he said. "And if it's really horrible, you come home, okay?"

That filled me with hope. An escape plan was always good. Man, my brother was right. When had we become so fearful?

Dad and I sat on the little train that would take us down to the boat, which would zip us across the channel to Naples.

I glanced at him. "How are you feeling?" I asked him.

"I'm in shock," he said. "I keep thinking about those bloody nails."

"Think of something else," I said. "Something fun."

"I can't," he whined. "Even thinking of something fun, like . . . getting hammered, brings me back to nails!"

Our trip turned out to be very smooth, the flight into Paris painless and brief. We retrieved our rental car, a lovely, crystal-blue Chrysler Sebring convertible. We dropped the top, and I realized I'd forgotten how much I missed driving. Dad had bought a vintage Triumph, which I accidentally demolished on Capri—the less said about that, the better—and I was stoked when he let me take the wheel. He wanted me to drive the convertible to St. Tropez.

I smoothed out one of the maps he'd kept in his office. He and Antonio had charted our travel route. Toppy covered his head with a Panama hat, put Perry Como (groan) into the CD player and I put the car in drive.

Dad put on his Italian sunglasses and prepared for a nap. I nudged him.

"What's this?" I pointed to a circle on the map.

"A fab little place Antonio says we should stop for lunch."

"Excellent."

I drove, with the sound of Perry Como's surprisingly soothing songs buoying my spirits. I pulled over at a rest stop at one point and checked my damn cell phone for messages. Still nothing from Hugh. I was beginning to feel like a stalker. One more text message to the guy and I'd be on the brink of bunny boilerdom.

After stopping and admiring the sea view, I pulled back onto the road. I had become intoxicated by the drive and realized we were about halfway to St. Tropez when I pulled into a small gas station to fill the tank. Toppy kept snoozing away. He came to life only when the smell of the cup of black coffee I bought from the station reached his nostrils.

"How far away are we from Plan-de-la-Tour?" he asked me, snatching my coffee out of my hands. He took a swig.

"About an hour and a half." It wasn't that the road was so long so much as very twisty and winding. It was also uphill and downhill, but very lovely.

"Okay," he said. "Wake me when we get there. Lunch is on me."

"You bet it is," I said, and fired up the car again.

"Your coffee tastes like shit," he said.

"Yeah, I know."

He started the CD player, and I got Perry Como again, but I didn't mind. I'd also listened to Nana Mouskouri, Max Bygraves, and Rosemary Clooney. Somehow the old-style music suited the red-roofed houses, ancient buildings, and drop-dead gorgeous water views below us.

I had been pretty close to my time frame. I took the turnoff for the town, staggered by the appearance of a pine forest and even mist. I could have been in Switzerland. Toppy awoke and pointed out the plane trees. We rolled into the charming inland town of Plan-de-la-Tour around two o'clock in the afternoon.

Toppy was bright-eyed and eager to find our way to the British-owned garden restaurant Antonio had recommended.

"A lot of British people live here," Toppy said. "They open these garden restaurants, and . . . oh look. There it is. How quaint."

He jumped out of the car before I'd even parked it. I pulled in beside a snazzy sports car and turned off the engine. The restaurant was a vine-covered house with antique furniture that spilled outside. The view of the ancient town, with its faraway glimpse of the sea, reminded me of an old movie Dad had forced me and Zeca to watch as kids, *Brigadoon*.

The restaurant turned out to be a local favorite. I'd had no idea that Johnny Depp and his partner, Vanessa, lived in the town, and according to Adrian, the owner of Connor's Garden, the couple came here often. I could see why. The food was sublime.

Toppy and I ate scallop risotto, steaks, and a fantastic dessert of profiteroles with chocolate fondant. We had a glass of the house wine and, afraid I'd sleep at the wheel, I had two cups of coffee.

Adrian was anxious. "Was everything okay?" he asked over and over. Toppy and I assured him everything had been perfect. Dad posed for photos with Adrian and a few of the guests.

A middle-aged Englishman approached me. "I watched you driving here."

"Excuse me?"

He gestured to a young man sitting at a table working on his cell phone with dexterous thumbs. "I hired him to drive me. I hired him and his car. I've seen all of Europe this way. I like handsome young men to drive me, except he irritates me. We were behind you for the last hour . . . you're a very good driver. Are you going to St. Tropez?"

"Er . . . ah . . . yeah. But—"

"What's your cell phone number? If you'd be willing to drive me around, I'll pay you well. You also get free meals, and I pay for gas."

"I . . . er . . ."

"Hey," my dad said, joining us. "What's going on?"

The man introduced himself. "Bruce Byron," he said, in a manner that suggested we should know who he was. Dad acted like he knew the name well. They chatted about England, the French Riviera, then Bruce repeated his offer to give me work. He had a certain thuggish glamour to him. Almost like the actor Jason Statham, with a few more years on him. I glanced over at Bruce's driver. He hadn't glanced up once, and his thumbs were extremely acrobatic.

"Give him your number, son. Keep your options open," Toppy said.

Bruce handed me what looked like an expensive pen and a piece of paper. I gave him my details.

"I'll be in touch," Bruce said, looking pleased with himself.

Outside the restaurant, Dad clapped his hand to my shoulder. "He's filthy bloody rich, mate. You can name your price."

"So *he* says."

"Alex," he said, taken aback. "Don't you know who Bruce Byron is?"

"No, I don't."

"He's a professional backgammon player. He's the reigning European champion. He makes bloody millions, and he's as eccentric as they come. He travels the world but always says driving is a gamble he won't make. He never likes to bet on things he isn't sure he'll win." Toppy smiled. I could tell he kinda liked Bruce Byron's style.

He stuck out his bottom lip and stared at our rental car. "I think this could be a good job for you, son. You don't get to drive in Capri since there are almost no bloody cars there. You've always been a damn good driver, and you'd get paid. You'd get to see some of the south of France."

"What about Hugh?"

"Ah. Well . . . about that . . ."

I gaped at him. "What haven't you told me?"

"He doesn't want to see you."

"What?" I almost exploded.

Dad lifted his shoulders.

"Why did you bring me out here?"

"I wanted the company, and I didn't exactly know *then* that he is so mad at you. His dad says he's met another guy."

"What?" I asked again. I felt like throwing myself over a cliff.

"You're both dumbasses," my dad said. "We thought . . . his dad and I thought with you here, showing sincere interest in Hugh, that he would, you know . . . change his mind. You know, son, soft-soap him a little."

"I can't do that."

"Of course you can. Or don't you love him enough?"

"I'm a bit like your mate Bruce Byron. I don't like to make bets I can't win."

Dad gave me a strange look. A mix of pity and love. "You love him enough, you can win the bet. Come on, son, let's get going."

We took off for St. Tropez, and I almost held my breath the whole way. I had such mixed emotions. My dad's romantic style was full-court press. I think I picked that up from him. It often landed us with disastrous results. I'd been realizing more and more that I liked chasing men . . . until I landed them. My heart belonged with Hugh. I just hated that feeling of not being in control.

As we got closer to the coast, Toppy sat up straighter beside me. "Wait. I booked us into a villa."

He produced a piece of paper, and we found the turnoff for the street indicated. The Villa Michel turned out to be a remarkable house overlooking Tahiti Beach.

"I picked this place because it's supposed to be the most risqué of all the beaches here," Toppy said.

The eight-bedroom mansion was a far cry from the poky house we had back in Capri. It had an electronic gate, for which Toppy had the access code, an alarm system and, once we found the house keys hidden in the lush foliage out front, it was a piece of paradise. Its white-walled decadence left both of us speechless. We wandered from room to room, taking in the antiques, the artwork, and lavish soft furnishings. Outside, both the warm lap pool in the tropical garden and the sun-drenched vista were almost blinding.

I kept discovering new rooms and was impressed with the wine cellar and humidor, which Toppy chortled over like a kid discovering a toy box full of unopened playthings.

He chomped on a cigar and grabbed a Cuban for the drive.

"How much did you spend on this?" I asked.

"Not as much as you'd think. Besides, it's the off-season."

There were giant plasma TVs in all the rooms, even the bathrooms, and kitchen. We were like little kids, swapping rooms, jumping on beds and finally choosing the ones we wanted.

I picked the bedroom that had an en-suite bathroom with a Jacuzzi. Once I won Hugh back, I planned to make the most of that feature.

"We can change rooms every night," Toppy said. "It comes with maid service. I've booked for two weeks. We'll have a blast."

He found a bottle of chilled champagne in the fridge and some caviar. I toasted him when he popped the bottle but took only a few sips of my drink. I was driving, after all, and besides, I didn't want to be blotto when I finally saw Hugh.

Back on the road, there was a traffic jam for the last twenty-minute drive down to St. Tropez.

I couldn't get over the cars or the view. The dizzying spectacle of the jumble of red-roofed houses, the bright blue ocean, endless boats moored in the harbor and the absolutely gorgeous, scantily clad people left and right made it a much slower journey. We made it down to the luxury beach town, Dad and I craning our necks as if we were at the scene of an accident.

"That's the restaurant."

Dad pointed to Café du Monde, across the road from the beach, its sidewalk tables spilling out toward the café next door.

And there was Hugh, standing out front.

He looked damn hot in white jeans and a blue-and-white-striped top. I nearly had an accident braking so suddenly. My heart pounded in my chest.

"Fuck me," Toppy said. "He doesn't look happy to see you."

Dad wasn't kidding. Hugh caught my glance and turned on his heel, disappearing inside the restaurant.

By the time I'd found parking and hoofed it into the joint, all that remained of him was the lingering scent of his aftershave. Tom Ford Grey Vetiver. Its distinctive mossy, nutmeg scent was unmistakable.

I wanted to run after the guy, but Dad was pulling me to the center of the café, introducing me to Hugh's parents.

Jack and Kathleen seemed like nice people, but I saw the hooded looks in their eyes. God knew what Hugh had said to them about me. His mom was a thin blonde with such big boobs, I was certain they were store-bought. She gave me a wide smile that didn't quite reach her eyes.

It was now close to five o'clock and starting to get dark. I was afraid I wouldn't see Hugh at all. His dad, an older, more lined version of Hugh, reminded me of his son with his good looks, thatch of shiny dark hair and blue eyes. He had Hugh's disarming smile.

"Where can I find him?" I asked.

Kathleen said nothing. Jack pointed to the beach. "He likes to watch the sunset."

I thanked him, turned, and ran. Toppy shouted something, but I didn't hear him. I was too busy darting between cars, taxis, and motorbikes. I spotted Hugh's T-shirt and followed the stripes. My heartbeat skidded in my chest, my palms getting sweatier.

He turned as if sensing me.

Hugh stopped, a kaleidoscope of emotions flittering across his features. I stared at his mouth, longing to kiss it. He had the sweetest mouth I'd ever seen on a man. I stepped forward.

His mouth opened but he didn't stop me. For a wonderful moment, I felt him moving closer. I kissed him. My hands moved to his silken hair. We drank from each other — until he pulled away from me, his face wet with tears.

"Fuck you," he said.

I pulled him closer. I felt his cock hardening against my belly. "Hugh . . . I love you so much."

"No. No . . . you can't say that."

"But I do. I love you."

My mouth sought and found his. Through my own blinding tears, I kissed him, Hugh returning all my passion. Then he broke away again.

"You can't do this," he screamed, pushing me away.

"I came here for you . . . to tell you how sorry I am."

"No," he said, backing away from me. He stumbled on the sand, and I went to him, helping him up. He sobbed and shrieked, people staring at us. I felt the tears falling from my eyes, down my chest as Hugh wrenched away from me.

"You're too late," he said. "I've met somebody else. I

don't want you anymore."

"Don't say that, baby. Please! Give me a chance," I said, dropping to my knees.

"Don't you fucking do this!" He tugged at his hair — then he was gone.

Oh my God. He ran away from me, and I was on my knees. A big fat loser.

So much for being relentless.

CHAPTER FOUR

I called my brother, who talked me off the emotional ledge on which I found myself. I paced the beach, trying not to hyperventilate.

"You haven't even begun to be relentless," he said. "If you love this guy, hang in there, Alex."

Easy for him to say. He was home, safe in his lover's arms, enjoying his siesta. At least, he had been until I called.

"Keep the faith," Zeca said. "I have a good feeling about this."

The evening deepened, stars twinkling in the sky and on the stretchy promenade. I'd never seen so many beautiful, happy people in my life. I remembered a time not so long ago when I was as carefree and fun. As I finished the call with Zeca and wandered back across the road, I tried to remind myself my life was not so terrible. I could be in much worse places, doing much worse things.

I could smell my man's aftershave again inside his parents' café. I knew he'd just been here. I'd never had such an awareness of a man's scent before, and it depressed me. I had all these bursting feelings and all these sensory perceptions for a man who didn't want me.

Toppy had gone off drinking with Jack, which didn't seem to make his wife very happy. She seemed less than thrilled to be left alone with me.

Their setup was quite different from ours. Café du Monde was a chocolate and coffee bar. The drinks came in different-shaped bowls. There were no meals, only snacks, but she had three guys who covered the bar area, two more waiting tables. I was surprised how packed it was.

I was about to leave, having received no word from Toppy when I'd called his cell phone.

"Have you tried hot white truffle chocolate?" Kathleen asked me.

I shook my head.

"Stay and have a cup," she said, the nicest she'd been to me since we'd arrived. She ordered the hot drinks from one of the waiters and found us a corner table. The hot chocolate arrived via a cute blond waiter. We eyed each other, but Kathleen didn't miss a trick. I was in enough trouble with her, so I just thanked the guy, wrapping my hands around the oval-shaped bowl. It fit perfectly in my palms as I sipped. Man, it was delicious. She left the table, returning with a small plate of biscotti.

"Homemade," she told me. I dunked a dark-chocolate-dipped one into my drink. Sublime.

"Toppy says you do well with your meals at Café Toppy," she said. "Is it hard work?"

I shrugged. "Yes, but my brother makes it look easy. He's a wonderful chef." I paused, wondering how he was getting along in the restaurant with Antonio's mom.

Kathleen prattled on about the restaurant business. She was full of questions.

"You have the same menu all day?"

"Yes," I said, "except for breakfast. Lunch and dinner are the same."

For a few minutes she stuck to the safe topic of food before saying, "You broke my son's heart."

"I didn't mean to. Honest."

My answer seemed to surprise her. "You're really upset."

I fiddled with the tablecloth.

"Stay there," she said. Her hand covered mine for a moment before she got up and barked a few orders to the waiters. The café was still thriving. When she came back, I thanked her for the drink.

"I feel like I'm taking up your time."

"Nonsense," she said. "I wanted the chance to get to know you. Hugh said you would try to charm me." Her eyes narrowed. "I don't get the sense you're trying too hard."

I smiled then. "I'm fresh out of charm. I had no idea until today that he didn't want to see me. So you see, we both got our hearts stomped on. What's his new boyfriend like?"

She paused as a different waiter came over with a platter of fried zucchini blossoms and two glasses of rosé. For the first time, I realized the whole tone of the place had changed. It was no longer a chocolate and coffee bar, but a wine bar. Almost every table held the fried blossoms and glasses of rosé.

"It's the speciality of St. Tropez." Kathleen raised her glass to me.

My heart froze. *Speciality.* A certain class of English people threw an extra I in the word. It was *specialty.*

I realized my mother had pronounced it the way Kathleen did, and I became gripped with the urge to flee.

"His boyfriend's all right. Not who I would have chosen for him," Kathleen said. I stayed in my seat. "Then again, you're not either. My son has been miserable these last couple of weeks."

"So have I." I'd done a bang-up job pretending the whole ugly incident on our last night together hadn't happened.

She didn't say anything.

"You think there's anything I can do to change his mind?" I asked.

"No."

She seemed to take way too much satisfaction in that. There seemed to be no reason to stay and put up with her barbed comments any longer. I didn't touch the wine. I thanked her for her time and excused myself. She looked startled.

"Where are you going?" she asked.

"No idea." Boy, was that the truth.

I walked outside. She didn't try to follow me. I tried Toppy again and was relieved when he answered.

"Hey, sunshine, how's it hangin'?"

"Are you drunk?" I asked.

"Gettin' there."

God, my dad . . . he knew how to have a good time.

"Listen, do whatever you want tonight. I'll get a taxi up to the house later . . . don't wait up. I hope to get lucky." He let loose a braying laugh.

I checked my watch. It was now seven p.m., and I wished this day to be long over. I crossed the street, retrieved the car and after several minutes of wrestling it from its tight parking spot, I headed back up the hill and over the rocky ridge toward Tahiti Beach. I fought off waves of emotion. I imagined Hugh to be with his boyfriend, and it hurt. Nausea rose in my throat, and I had to pull over and throw up. I jumped out of the car so I didn't barf all over the new interior of the convertible. It was awful. I felt like crap when I got back inside the car. I needed a diversion. My fingers shook as I pressed the CD player for music and got Rosemary Clooney.

The song she was singing was 'I Get Along Without You Very Well.' God was having way too much fun with me.

I found my way back home, surprised the streets were so well lit. I thanked my lucky stars that Dad had left the gate code instructions in the car. I let myself onto the property and unlocked the front door, feeling a pang of guilt that Toppy and I had forgotten to set the burglar alarm. I felt so unhappy, I took a long shower and went to bed. I turned on the plasma TV and plugged my cell phone into its charger.

I tried desperately not to remember the conversation I'd had with Kathleen. Mothers normally loved me. I was glad that I didn't feel any attraction for her, but I didn't even *like* her. It was all for the best.

My cell phone rang. I lunged for it, tearing up when I saw it was Zeca.

"What happened?" he asked. I muted the TV, told him everything and was buoyed by his protective fury.

"Who the fuck is *she* to talk to you like that?" He spent half an hour convincing me not to fly home the next morning. "I'd stay away from the café, but leave him a message. Tell him you're thinking about him."

My brother's advice seemed good. I did as he suggested and ten seconds after I'd called Hugh, my cell phone rang. I thought it was him, but it turned out to be Bruce Byron.

"I need a driver for tomorrow. I have a big backgammon game at a club in St. Tropez. I'll pay you two hundred dollars to pick me up at my hotel at nine o'clock in the morning. I have a meeting in the afternoon too. We'll be back around five."

That sounded pretty good to me. I took down his details and figured I could always stop by the café in the evening and let Hugh know I was still around. As my brother was fond of pointing out, Hugh had braved sharks for me. I could brave his fake-breasted mother.

Toppy didn't come home, and by the morning I was feeling well rested after a good night's sleep. I left a message on Toppy's voicemail with the instructions for the gate and house codes then I set the alarm and drove back to St. Tropez. It really was a beautiful place. I had realized as I mapped the Chateau de la Messardiere that it was in the countryside. I almost missed the turnoff but found it high in the hills in the middle of a huge estate.

It was impressive. I'll say that. There were breathtaking views of the ocean and as soon as I arrived, Bruce shook my hand. He was dressed in a silk robe. His private valet had led me to the terrace outside Bruce's suite. He offered me coffee and breakfast, and I said yes to everything, wolfing down eggs, pancakes, bacon, and several cups of coffee. Bruce wandered back and forth, making several calls. When he was ready to leave, he appeared in black trousers and an understated charcoal shirt. Everything about him oozed money.

"I've been looking forward to this match," he said.

"My dad tells me you're the European champion. I'm sorry, I had no idea."

Bruce grinned. "No problem. I take it you're not a gambling man?"

"Not unless you consider my track record in the dating world a gamble."

He laughed. "A good-looking guy like you shouldn't be having dating trouble."

His searing look was disquieting. I rose from the table feeling underdressed in my jeans and shirt.

"You look fine," he said when I mentioned it. "You're young and handsome. You'd look sexy in a potato sack, for God's sake."

Was he gay? There didn't seem to be anything behind his words. He was being kind. I watched him walk back into his room to retrieve a black leather bag. He was slim, in pretty good shape but not overly toned. His wide shoulders tapered to a trim waist, where his charcoal shirt was tucked into his trousers.

"Let's go." He asked me to open the trunk and place a suit jacket inside. He then directed me to a hotel down by Pampelonne Beach.

"Some people say this is the best beach in St. Tropez."

That was the second time I'd heard that about the south coast in two days. I guess everybody had their favorites.

"You a backgammon fan?" he asked.

"I play but my dad is a terrible loser, and he taught me."

Bruce grinned. "We'll have to play sometime."

He alternately conducted phone calls in three different languages on his cell and played backgammon with himself on a portable hand-held unit. I studied him in the rearview mirror. He had close-cropped sandy hair and a kind of hardness to his features I found intriguing. He caught my gaze and pointed to a massive, sprawling, Mediterranean-style hotel, more old-worldly than anything I'd seen so far except for the chateau where Bruce was staying.

A small brass plaque on a Spanish column announced it as the Majestique, and I drove through the gates to tropical splendor.

"You can come and watch, or you can pick me up at two," he said.

"I'd like to watch. I've never seen a professional back-gammon tournament before."

It must have been the right answer. He waited for me to open his door then asked me to pop the trunk. He handed me his black Boss jacket.

"Put this on, please." The jacket felt luxurious and expensive against my body. "Nice," he said.

We walked through the hotel once I'd relinquished the car to the valet. People stopped and stared, a few rushed over and wished Bruce good luck.

"Do you need me to do anything?" I asked him in a low voice as a woman with long, tanned legs and a short office suit escorted us up two floors to a private suite.

"No." He looked surprised. "Thanks for asking though."

"Nothing at all?" I asked.

"I'd like you to be quiet in the room, no texting, talking on your phone or . . ." He paused. I waited for him to continue, but he didn't. His attention was now on the woman wishing him a good game as she opened the door. I was a little shocked at the controlled chaos inside the lush suite.

About twenty people were assembled, two of them women. I recognized one of them, a bottle-blonde actress I'd seen on TV shows. In spite of the smiles and friendliness between the players, there was nervousness and a strong ripple of fear in the room. The blonde shook my hand with unusual force.

"Well, aren't you the cat's meow," she said, lighting a cigarette. People in Europe smoked everywhere, but it still managed to surprise me.

"Thank you," I said, for want of something better to say.

She seemed to assess me and decided I wasn't worth flirting with. I sure hoped her *tatas* were fake because there was something sexy and vulnerable about her, especially since she'd rejected me as an object of desire and focused her gaze on a decrepit guy in a beret.

She thinks he has money.

A crisply uniformed waiter asked what I would like to drink. I ordered coffee, which he brought back right away. The blonde actress breezed through the first round of play, beating an old French man who cussed at her. The guy in the beret lost to her next. Bruce played on another side of the room, winning easily. They seemed destined to face one another. I was surprised at how entertaining just watching the game was. The players took a break for lunch, and it was only then that the waiters hurried around to everyone.

"Have whatever you want," Bruce said. He tilted his head, and I followed him outside. Until that moment I hadn't realized there were balconies attached to the rooms.

"You handled Blondie very well," he said, lighting a cigarette and sipping a macchiato with a twist the waiter handed him seconds after he'd ordered it.

"Thanks." I dropped my voice. "She's an actress, isn't she?"

He nodded. "With a fearsome gambling problem." He peered into the room through the open balcony door for a moment. "She owes several casinos around the world quite a bit of money. She's here trying to win, so she can pay some of them back."

"Will you let her win?"

He smiled at me. "No."

Bruce encouraged me to have some lunch. "It's part of the deal, and their food is excellent. I'm going to make some calls. I have one final game in an hour, and we'll be finished by two. Then I have an appointment. If you need to make some calls, please feel free. Once you're back in the room, you can't."

"Just like Vegas," I said. "No cell phones."

"Right."

He slipped back inside. When he passed by, I tried to inhale his scent. He smelled of soap. Clean. Despite the few puffs on the cigarette in his hand.

I stayed on the patio and perused the lunch menu. I shouldn't have been hungry, but I was. I ordered a nicoise salad and finished my coffee. Nobody talked to each other although I caught plenty of smiles around the patio. I checked through my cell phone messages and texts. Nothing. Not even from my dad. I called him.

"Where are you?" he asked.

"At Pampelonne Beach with Byron."

"Ah."

"Where are *you*, Dad?"

He chuckled. "In bed with a beautiful woman."

Holy crap. Did he really want to get into more female trouble?

"What time are you through?" he asked.

"Around five."

"I'll call you, and you can pick me up."

"Good deal."

I toyed with the idea of calling Hugh. Oh, what the hell. I texted *I miss you*. Somehow it made me feel better. It made me feel . . . relentless. I got the feeling if Bruce Byron wanted something, he'd go after it. He'd fight for it.

I texted Hugh again, apparently locating my inner daredevil. This time I wrote, *I mean it*. I switched off my phone and went inside.

By the time I returned to the tournament, the actress had lost and was leaving the suite with Jackie O-style sunglasses that didn't quite hide her devastation. She glanced in my direction, but I couldn't tell if she was looking at me. Her nose was red, and it twitched like a bunny's. I felt awful for her.

I watched, my palms turning sweaty, as Bruce threw the dice. He was an excellent gambler because he gave nothing away. He was lucky with doubles and moved his pieces with deftness. The elderly Frenchman who'd lost earlier sat beside me. I could feel his tension as well as my own.

I stole a glance at Bruce's opponent. He was a voluble Greek player who looked stricken when he made a bad call, separating two of his discs and having them both confiscated by Bruce. He tried hard to get back on the board, but Bruce was already removing pieces from the game. He won, and his opponent looked pissed.

"It's not over yet," the Greek said.

Bruce laughed. "*À plus tard*," he responded. "Until later." The two men shook hands, and I detected no hard feelings.

Bruce left on a high. We walked outside the hotel, and he studied a piece of paper he extracted from his briefcase as we waited for the car.

"I need to be at this hotel for a meeting. I shouldn't be more than a few hours. You can wait for me or come back."

"Which would you prefer?"

His mouth twitched into a smile. "I always think that a handsome young man is a wonderful thing when I gaze upon him, Alex, but in this instance, I'll be too busy dealing with business. Why don't you come back?"

"Okay." So I got the feeling he *was* gay, but as far as I could tell, his comments were benign. I dropped him at the Hotel Lou Cagnard. It was a slice of pure Provence with its biscuit-colored walls and dark blue trim. We pulled past an array of palm trees.

"Pick me up at five," Bruce said as I held the door for him. He didn't look at me, and I sensed tension.

"Should I wish you luck?" I asked.

He turned and looked at me. "No. I never need luck, Alex, but thank you."

Back in the car, I pondered my next move. I called Dad and got his voicemail. I decided to go home and sit by the pool. It was closer than St. Tropez beach and I liked the idea of sun-baking nude, not that I couldn't have done that in St. Tropez.

I got home, stripped off, swam for a bit and lounged on a deckchair. I could get used to this life. I texted Hugh. I was beginning to enjoy my own dementedness.

Lying in the sun naked. The sky is blue. The water would be perfect if you were in it.

I dropped the phone to the grass and stared up at the lazily drifting wisps of clouds. I dozed off, awoke in time to shower and redress and was at the hotel by five.

Bruce seemed preoccupied. I drove him back to his chateau, doing a fine job, I thought, of remembering all the streets and weird little turns. He must have thought so, too, because he complimented me on my skills before handing me some euros. I was surprised to find more than our agreed-upon amount.

"I like you, Alex. I have a question. I just agreed to compete in a high-stakes game in Monte Carlo tomorrow. It will involve a helicopter ride and overnight stay. Of course, I would pay your expenses, and you'd have your own five-star suite."

"You need a driver there?"

"Of course. I don't want to think about having a stranger drive me around, a stranger who, perhaps, is paid to make me run late."

"Do people do that kind of stuff?"

"You have no idea."

"Wow."

"Alex, I trust you. I think we're a good fit."

I'd never been to Monte Carlo, and the idea filled me with wonderment. "Yes," I said simply.

"Splendid. This time, wear a suit. See you at ten o'clock in the morning. Have a nice evening."

"You too, sir." I opened his door and let him out. I wondered what he'd do with his evening . . . and then wondered why I cared.

I drove away from the chateau and called Dad.

"Come get me," he said. "My boys are in agony. I think I overdid the sex."

His boys? Oh boy. He gave me his address. He was off the beach in St. Tropez. I drove down the hill, listening to Rosemary Clooney tell me 'It's Bad for Me.'

I collected Toppy, who looked none the worse for wear, though slightly bow-legged.

"She put an elastic band around my frank and beans," he said as soon as he got in the car. "You ever heard of such a thing?"

"Sounds painful if it's on too long. You've never used a cock ring?"

"A what?" He stared at me. "I'm strictly a meat and potatoes guy, in the sack and out of it," he said.

"Are you in pain?"

"Nah. Just need a rest." I glanced at the house where he'd come from. It was nothing like ours . . . or the chateau.

"Are you hungry?" he asked. "Let's pop into your boy-friend's caf, then get some dinner." I loved that he pro-nounced it *caf*, the English way.

At St. Tropez's beachfront, things were in full swing.

"I kinda met a nice woman last night," Toppy said. "She made my guys very, very happy. The rubber band thing was weird . . . but hot. It's pretty exciting stuff."

"Christ, Dad. You are a horny old goat."

"Aren't I though?"

He seemed so proud of himself, all I could do was laugh.

We parked, and I found myself shaking as we walked to-ward the caf. He stopped me. "For Christ's sake, son, what's the matter with you? Why are you nervous?"

"He hates me, remember?"

Dad scoffed. "No, he doesn't hate you. He's playing hard to get."

"Yeah . . . well, we'll see." I had my hopes up and was brutally wounded when Hugh vanished out the backdoor the moment we arrived.

"Did you take ugly pills or something?" Toppy asked. "He's acting a bit over the top, don't you think?"

I couldn't respond. I was too upset.

Kathleen didn't seem happy to see either of us. Her face fell when Toppy and Jack took off for a quick round of drinks.

That left me alone with her again. I turned on my heel and left.

"Dad," I shouted, catching up with him. "Are we having dinner?"

"Maybe not," he said. Man, everybody was dumping me left and right.

I drove home, stopping along the way for Thai takeout at Oth Sombath. It was an elegant restaurant, but I didn't want to dine alone. Somehow, Thai takeout in the middle of St. Tropez seemed weird and funny at the same time. I ordered spring rolls, green papaya salad, shrimp macaroons with pineapple sauce. I fell in love with every dish on the menu. I had just settled on one more thing—red tuna with basil and lemongrass—when I caught a whiff of cologne.

Hugh.

I turned, but it wasn't him. Man, I was ready to leap into total mind-snapping obsession.

The hostess sweet-talked me into dessert. She suggested banana spring rolls with coffee ice cream and red wine ginger sauce.

"I'll throw in an order of the caramelized coconut in a banana leaf," she said. "You won't believe how good it is."

Boy, it was my lucky day. I loved free stuff.

As I waited for my food, I sent Hugh another text. *I fucking love you so much, you are all I think about.*

There. Let him put that in his pipe and smoke it.

Back home I ate dessert first, sitting in my bed. I was afraid of the ice cream melting. I needn't have worried. The most expensive takeout I'd ever had in my life came with such amazing packaging, including dry ice for the dessert. The only thing better would have been feeding it to Hugh.

I texted him and told him so. I'd gotten comfortable with the idea of being a bunny boiler. I enjoyed sending him constant updates. My mad pot was bubbling on the stove. Hugh would either cave in, or he'd have me arrested.

Mean Girls, our favorite movie, came on TV. Huh. I texted and told him so.

I mowed through all my food and realized that my bed hadn't been made. I thought Toppy said the house came with maid service. Not that it mattered.

Sucking banana cream from my fingers, I sank into the pillows on my bed and contemplated the last bite of spring roll. Before I knew it, I'd drifted to sleep.

I awoke at the crack of dawn to the sound of Toppy throwing rocks at my window. I found myself surrounded by empty cartons and my mouth felt disgustingly furry.

"All right, all right," I shouted and stumbled to the door to let him in.

Toppy was pretty drunk. He fell face first to the grass outside the house. I dragged him inside, hauled him to his bed and removed his shoes. Then I dozed another hour and prepared myself for my trip to Monte Carlo. I was excited about it, and by the time I left to pick up Bruce, Dad was still sleeping on top of the bed where I'd left him. I wrote him a note explaining where I was going and took off, anticipating my big day out in the richest little municipality in the world.

I collected Bruce, who came out of the chateau as soon as I arrived.

"Have you had breakfast?"

"Not yet. Only coffee."

"Good. I know a place in Monte Carlo. We'll be there in an hour." He paused. "You look very handsome this morning, Alex."

He let me stow his overnight bag in the trunk and directed me to a heliport about two miles behind the chateau. Parking the car in a field beside two others, I raised the top and locked up, following Bruce with our bags.

I had never been on a chopper before, but the trip was dazzling and brief. Bruce kept pointing things out to me, like the castle in Monaco, the casinos and his favorite haunts. A limo picked us up at the heliport and drove us to a car rental agency.

"Pick out whatever you want," Bruce said to me.

"No, I want whatever you want."

His gaze swiveled to mine and for a brief moment, I detected some sexual heat from him that went right to my cock. Boy, I was sure hard-up to even think the guy was coming on to me.

He picked out a sleek, silver Mercedes E350 Cabrio. The convertible had twelve miles on it. I was in love. I dropped the top and let him into the backseat, putting our bags in the trunk. He directed me to the restaurant he'd mentioned.

Breakfast at a little hole in the wall on Rue Saint François de Paule was amazing, the croissants we downed the flakiest, most buttery things I'd ever eaten. He talked me into sampling them with a mixture of fresh fruits the restaurant pressed by hand.

"So, are you seeing anyone?" he asked me.

I shrugged. "I was. I came here . . . well, to St. Tropez, but he's got a new boyfriend."

"That's too bad."

I would have asked if *he* was seeing anyone, but suddenly I didn't want to know.

"Have another coffee," he said, apparently reading my mind. "We have time."

Two cups of coffee later, I felt like a butterball.

We drove to our hotel, the Port Palace, right on the ocean overlooking the Mediterranean. Our adjoining suites were sumptuous and modern. Mine had an unusual, arched leather recliner with a plush throw strewn across it, poised at the perfect angle to watch the water.

The suite was amazing.

Bruce stood in the doorway, watching me. "You like it?"

"I love it, Bruce. It's like a fantasy."

"Good, I'm glad."

He walked toward me. "You asked me yesterday if there was anything you could do for me and you kinda put me on the spot. Since then, I've had time to think."

"Oh yes?" Why did I feel a surge of sexual fire? I felt so turned on by this guy all of a sudden. "What can I do for you?" My voice came out all feeble and croaky.

"I like to suck cock before I play."

"Oh my God." I'd been pretty sure he was gay, but his words still shocked me. "You're saying you want to suck *my* cock?

"Why do you think I like young, hot guys to drive me around?"

He dropped a kiss on my chin and unbuckled my belt. "You're the first one in a long time that I've had trouble keeping my hands off. You're a hot guy, Alex."

He was rubbing my crotch and, in spite of myself, I was getting even hotter for Bruce.

"I know you're all tormented over some guy, but he's busy getting laid. You'd be getting off, helping me win my match and . . ." His disarming smile almost made me come in my pants. "I give the best blowjobs in the business."

Damn. That was quite a boast, especially when I was beyond horny — and heartbroken.

"He would never have to know." Bruce's smoky eyes filled with lust. "Having a man suck off your cock will keep your hormones in check and, of course, you'd be making me extremely happy."

I was still getting over the idea of Bruce wanting to suck me. He kept rubbing my cock head through my dress pants. I didn't have the power to resist him. He didn't want to fuck me. He just wanted to suck me, and boy, did I want the best blowjob in the business. His breath grew shallower as his fingers pulled my cock out of my pants, and the way he teased the head with his tongue . . . I gazed down at him, watching the affectionate kiss he gave it.

He gave me a gentle shove, and I fell back on the recliner.

Its shape had my crotch jutting right up to him. His fingers worked to pull down my pants, and I passed a hand across my eyes. I tried not to think about Hugh; the only thing that worked was pretending Bruce *was* Hugh.

Bruce hadn't been lying. He got me hard, his mouth sucking me in all the way. He sucked cock as if his life depended on it. I found myself responding. I leaned up on my elbows to watch and was surprised when he released me.

"You got a nice, juicy cock there, sweetheart," he said. He ran his tongue around my balls. I was surprised at the reverent way he sucked them in, increasing the pressure with his lips and tongue. He handled my ball sac like it was a pair of dice in his hands. I felt an explosion of pleasure.

"Suck me," I said, knowing I was about to come. He put his mouth back on me. He kept it there until I flooded his throat, his thumbs swirling back and forth in crazy-eights on my ball sac. I came so hard, I almost blacked out. I fell back on the recliner.

"That was so good," he said. "I'll win today for sure."

And he did.

I sat in the backgammon room, watching him play. When he shook the dice in his hand, I caught his gaze. I had a weird feeling he was thinking about me . . . well, my balls, to be more precise. I felt myself getting hard . . . and hot.

He won all his matches and picked up his check. As we left the club, he kept his hand on the small of my back. We waited for the car to be brought around.

"There's one more place we have to go, but I want to make a pit stop."

"Okay," I said.

"Put the top up," he instructed. I watched him tip the valet driver, and as we got into the vehicle, Bruce leaned forward. "Find somewhere pretty but secluded to park."

My cock grew hard instantly. I found a place on a deserted cliff road and parked.

"Pretty man, get back here with me," he said.

I switched off the ignition and climbed into the backseat of the Mercedes. His hand was on my crotch before I even got to him. In the soft, late-afternoon sun, I could see the lusty expression on his face. He settled me on the seat beside him.

"Get comfy," he said.

I did, waiting for him to release my cock. This time he took my shoes off, massaging my feet. He worked the balls of my feet, his knuckles pressing into them. I cried out. It hurt so good. He took my socks off, unbuckled my belt, and drew down my pants. I panicked a bit when I found myself naked from the waist down, but when his tongue tip touched my cock, my ass flew off the seat. He caught me up in his hands, his face moving to my ass. He licked and sucked me like nobody had, except for Hugh.

He put his shoulders into the business of pleasuring of me. My legs opened up to him. I had one foot on his shoulder, the other poised on the headrest of the passenger seat. I stroked his almost-bald head and begged for release.

"Make me come," I whispered. He kept his tongue inside my ass, his fingers stroking my cock. I fingered my nipples, in shock that my boss was giving me such an incredible thrill.

As I started to shoot, his mouth came off me. Through half-closed eyes I watched his tongue move to my cock and felt his thumb inside my ass, warm and wanted. He sucked me as I came, and I cried out. His mouth tightened, his sucking sounds driving me crazy. I flooded his throat.

As soon as I finished, he released me with a pop. He took his face away and upended me, spitting my juices onto my ass. He sucked me again, my ass feeling slick and hot. He still had his thumb plunging in and out of me. He took it out and sucked it, looking at me.

I wished I could let him fuck me. I felt his cock hardening against my thigh.

"Can I fuck you, Alex?"

I shook my head. I couldn't. Just couldn't. He took his time sucking me, bringing me to the brink again and again. When he finally let me come, I was a wreck. I was sobbing, begging the man for release.

The bliss I experienced was intense and powerful. I saw fireworks in my mind, then a wall of blackness. I think I actually passed out. I felt his mouth at my ear.

"Didn't I tell you?" he asked. "Didn't I tell you I'd give you the blowjob from hell?"

I nodded and felt his mouth on mine. I kissed him, but in the next breath, I said, "I have to go back to St. Tropez in the morning."

He didn't seem to mind. We slept in our own rooms. He didn't try to come to me. I knew *I* could, and would, resist him, but I didn't want any aggravation. He gave me none. I had trouble sleeping in spite of coming three times that evening. And then my cell phone rang.

It was my dad.

"I just spoke to Hugh's dad. He tells me Hugh's upset because you stopped texting him all day."

That was true. I'd been consumed with my boss.

I put a call through to Hugh. I got his voicemail, so I sent a text.

Nothing.

I was so mad, I knocked at the adjoining door of my suite and Bruce opened it. He was naked and sporting a hard, huge cock. Lying naked on his rumpled bed . . .

Was Hugh.

CHAPTER FIVE

"What the fuck?" I screamed.

Hugh sat up. "What are you doing in here naked?"

"You . . . He . . ." My head snapped back and forth between them. "Wait . . . is *this* your new boyfriend?" I asked him.

Hugh slowly nodded.

Bruce laughed. "You should see your faces!"

I'd been had.

Hugh's face turned chalk-white. He turned to Bruce. "You fucked him?"

"Naw, babe. He wouldn't let me. Sucked him off good though."

Hugh glared at me. "You said you loved me."

"I *do* love you. I've been so fucking depressed. I went all the way to St. Tropez to see you, and you run from me every time you see me. Your mom said you didn't want to see me, so I took this job. I've texted you. I've left messages. You've never returned a single one!"

He stared at me, his gaze cutting back to Bruce. "You seduced him? You knew what I was going through. I trusted you . . . and you . . . seduced him?"

For the first time since I'd met him, Bruce looked uncomfortable. "Come on, babe, I wanted to see what all the fuss was about. You talk about this guy like he's Jesus Christ reincarnated . . . he's the most selfish lover I ever met!"

"Wait a minute. You said you wanted to suck me off. That it's your good luck thing. I was horny and . . . and . . . heart-

70

broken. I said yes. So sue me! I never led you on. It was on you, Bruce."

"You said the same thing to me," Hugh whispered. "You cheated on me!"

I opened my mouth, but he wasn't talking to me. He was talking to Bruce.

"You're my whole life," I said to Hugh. "I'm sorry this happened. I'm sorry I'm a stupid guy."

Hugh said nothing. Hard glints showed in his eyes.

Bruce strode toward him. "I can explain."

"Nothing to explain," Hugh said. "You're a jerk." He got out of the bed and ran to the bathroom, slamming the door behind him.

"I quit," I said to Bruce. "I'm going home right now."

"Don't be an idiot. We'll all go back together. The chopper's leaving in a couple of hours. Let me talk to him."

I nodded and backed out of the room. Once again, it had all gone horribly wrong. I cursed myself for letting my loneliness and stupid hormones get the better of me. I wanted to be on that chopper, to be near Hugh. I needed a chance to talk to him.

Would Hugh ever forgive me?

I waited for hours in my room. I heard them making love, and it nearly broke me. Bruce was a cruel man; he wanted me to hear. When they came to get me, to say the drive was the most awkward one of my life, was an understatement. I was driving the man I loved as he made out with the man who'd seduced me and taken Hugh from me. I have no idea how I didn't crash the car.

We returned the rental car, and a limo took us to the helipad. I knew the chopper ride would be brief. I think they both got off on making out right in front of me. Back at the heliport in St. Tropez, I retrieved the car. Plonking our bags in the trunk, I wondered what the hell I was going to do next.

I dropped them at the chateau and Bruce tossed a wad of money in my lap.

"I don't want it." I flicked it back to him.

"Take it. You earned it."

"I don't care. I don't want your money. The only thing I want from you is my man."

He didn't seem to know how to respond.

"Sorry you're quitting," he said as I opened the trunk and handed them their bags. I caught Hugh's gaze. I was amazed to see abject misery there. Well, good. Because I felt like hell, too.

As soon as they walked toward the entrance of the hotel, I headed home. Man, Toppy had made a mess of things the last day or so and there was definitely no maid service. I threw out the takeout crap that was in my room and Toppy's empty pizza cartons and beer bottles and then fell into bed. I'd sleep and decide what to do with the rest of my life.

"Alex."

"Huh?" Dad was shaking me awake. "What time is it?"

"Three in the afternoon. What happened in Monte Carlo?"

I sat up, feeling a little disoriented. "Have you heard anything?"

He shoved my legs aside and perched on my bed. "No, son. I got a phone call from Zeca. He said he was worried about you."

I swallowed hard. "It was a disaster."

"Come on, tell me what happened."

He was dressed in a T-shirt and Bermuda shorts. He looked like he was relaxed and tanned. I hated putting any stress on him.

"You're going to hate me."

"Alex, nothing could be worse than you killing my Triumph and I still love you in spite of it. Let's have some coffee, and you'll tell me all about it."

I nodded. I had no idea what to do next. My attempts at being relentless had so far been pretty craptastic. In the kitchen, he popped bread in the toaster and made fresh coffee. We sat on stools around the kitchen island. It felt nice to have my father fuss over me . . . and then he listened to my tale of woe.

"Wait a second . . . Bruce Byron's going out with Hugh? *He's* his boyfriend?"

I shrugged. "Apparently."

"And he seduced you?"

"Yeah."

"The bastard." He paused. "How was it?"

I shook my head. "Dad . . . it was pretty . . . amazing."

"Damn. Bruce Byron's gay? Do you like him?"

"I did . . . but not like that. I liked hanging out with him. I thought he was cool and interesting."

Dad refilled our coffee cups. "And you came back with them this morning?"

"Yeah, and they kept making out in front of me."

He pulled a face. "How tacky."

"Tell me about it."

"So what happens now?"

I looked at him. "I was hoping *you* could tell me that. I feel like such a loser."

"Did he pay you?"

"He did, but I tossed his money back to him. I told him the only thing I wanted from him was Hugh."

Dad grinned. "Excellent. What did Hugh say to that?"

"He looked miserable."

"This is some fucked-up bullshit."

"Yeah. You can say that again."

Toppy toyed with his coffee spoon. "I think it's time for a family conference." He tossed the spoon into sink. It fell with a clatter on top of stacked dishes. "Say," he said. "I thought this joint was supposed to come with maid service?"

"So did I."

"Well, I'll track down the owner and see what's what. In the meantime, you and I are going down to that damn café to have a few words with Hugh and his parents."

"Dad . . ." I shook my head. "I'm a big boy now. You can't go to the headmaster's office and protect me anymore."

He stared at me. "They want me to sink a bunch of money into their café. They won't get one red penny out of me until Hugh talks to you."

"That's the help they want? Money?"

"Yeah. Money. And money talks. And so do we. We're a big family of talkers." He got off his stool and did a little soft shoe on the tiled floor. "If we can't bullshit our way through this, we'll dazzle 'em with our moves."

Good old Toppy. He always made me laugh.

My cell phone rang. I could hear my Lady Gaga ringtones from the kitchen. To my amazement, when I finally raced into my bedroom and retrieved it, it was Hugh.

I'd missed his call and waited to see if he left a message. Toppy stood in my doorway.

"It's him, isn't it?"

I glanced up as my phone rang again. "Hugh," I said as I took the call.

"We need to talk." Hugh sounded strange.

"Are you okay?" I asked.

"No, I'm not." His voice sounded thick with emotion. "This is *your* fault all this happened. You fucking hurt me!"

"I know." I sat on my bed, the phone pressed hard to my ear. More than anything, I wanted him right there with me. I

74

wanted to explain. For a guy who had a lot to say, I was tongue-tied. "Hugh, there's so many things I want to tell you, but can't. I love you. You're the first man I've said that to, ever."

Aware of my father tiptoeing away from the room, I fought off my own tears as Hugh sobbed on the other end of the line.

"Baby, I know I screwed up."

He said nothing. A moment later he ended the call.

"Well?" Toppy's head poked around my doorframe.

"He hung up on me."

My father frowned. He got the murderous look on his face that he got when kids at school bullied me for being 'queer.' I hadn't minded the word so much because ten years ago in England, it didn't have the same vicious connotation it did now. What I minded was the hypocrisy. Half the guys in my class were having each other. I was a virgin and had crushes from afar. Maybe I didn't dig chicks, I'd thought. Maybe I *was* queer after all.

Dad had gone to my headmaster, who'd refused to intervene, saying it would cause more harm than good. Dad took me and Zeca out of the school that day. We ended up at a much better school and did well for ourselves.

We were both on the fast track to our A Levels when our mother abducted us.

Looking back, I'd say that Zeca and I were both pretty innocent kids. We were so pleased to see her show up at school after she'd run off and left us the previous year. She cried a bunch, hugging and kissing us. We were teenagers, not little kids, so nobody checked whether she was supposed to pick us up—or not. I wanted to know why Dad wasn't coming with us. Every kid, no matter what their age, wants to see their parents back together. In that moment, when she held me and told me she loved me, I would have forgiven her *anything*.

But she got angry. It frightened me. I wanted to call Dad to let him know we were going with her, but her behavior became even more bizarre. She claimed Toppy knew she was picking us up. Zeca didn't believe her. He was frightened and wanted to run. He'd grabbed my hand. That's when she said, *I have a surprise*.

She took us to the train station. We'd climbed aboard . . . and minutes later the train crashed.

I was okay. She was *not* okay. And Zeca nearly died.

Surprise!

I've disliked surprises ever since. Toppy understood. He's never so much as popped a champagne cork without some advance notification.

I sat there on my bed, realizing just how long I'd been carrying the damage Mum had done to us. I'd lived with an emotional limp.

"All this time, Dad, I didn't think the train crash affected me. Mum was hurt. Zeca was hurt . . . I thought I was okay, but their injuries were on the outside. I-I never stopped to think because nothing was broken on my body, that inside, I wasn't a fucking mess."

"I know, son." His voice was quiet.

Zeca and I had talked about it. He'd tried to make me see. It was only now, when it was still and quiet that I saw it all. My dad had never done anything unexpected after that. He talked for two years about his plans before he left England to open his restaurant in Capri. Zeca and I had successful careers in the financial sector as stock brokers, but we missed him, and he us. The three of us were a team.

"He surprised me, Dad. When Hugh asked me to marry him, I felt trapped. I felt like I was in that bloody train all over again. It was all I could hear. This great big bloody noise. Like a train whistle blowing."

My father's expression turned to dismay.

"All I could think was . . . run."

He blinked. "Does Hugh know what happened?"

I couldn't remember ever having told him. I didn't think it was important. Until Zeca fell in love, he'd squashed the memories, too.

Dad looked lost in thought. Was he remembering his lost and crushed teens? I remember Dad turning up at the train station. I remember the look on his face when he found us. I had never realized how much he loved us until the moment I saw his grief and his heartbreak.

"I'm going to fix this," he said. "Give me two minutes."

For longer than two minutes, I sat, the dark thoughts settling like mud in my soul.

"Antonio knows," Dad said. His voice startled me. "He came and talked to me one night. He had a lot of questions."

"I bet he did. He's a cop."

"No, son. He's a man in love." He came and sat beside me, putting his arm around my shoulders. "Your problem is that you're afraid to trust. You loved Hugh from the beginning. I don't know when you decided you didn't deserve love, Alex, but you do. I meant it when I said this trip was about bringing you two together. Sometimes we all need a push, some gentler than others."

"Did you need to push Zeca?"

His smile reappeared. "I did." His smile faltered again. "He thought he would die without Antonio. That's when I knew they belonged together. Hugh's dad and I have talked . . . there's something you don't know about Jack. He's gay, and he's finally coming out of the closet. So Hugh's had a lot to deal with."

"Does Kathleen know?"

Dad nodded.

Heck, no wonder she was so unhappy. "What a mess," I said.

"Not really." Dad grinned at me. "She was my girlfriend when I was a teenager. I think . . ." He lifted his hands.

"She was?" I gaped at him. "You mean Mum wasn't your first love?"

"What, are you nine?" he asked. "Of course not."

"So you're . . . what? In love with her?"

"No. In like. We're sort of fumbling around."

"Oh, my ears." I clapped my hands over them. "I don't want to know about this. Wait . . . is she the one who put the elastic band around your . . . er . . . guys?"

"Hell no. That was Francesca. She's a delectable little local dish."

"You're incorrigible. And you think *I* don't trust love."

"Holy cow," Dad said. "You might have something there." He looked contemplative for a moment.

"You're flirting with danger, Dad. You're canoodling with this Francesca and what are you doing with Kathleen?"

His cheeks reddened. "Getting to know each other again. Hey, it was Jack's idea."

"I bet it was. Nice way to assuage his guilt by hooking her up with you."

Toppy looked astonished. "I hadn't thought of it that way." His bottom lip stuck out. "Jack and his lover want to take over the restaurant."

"And you and Kathleen will do what?"

"Go back to Capri . . . if it works out."

"She hates me."

"No, she doesn't. She's protective. Like me. Believe me, I gave Hugh a bit of the hairy eyeball myself over you."

"The hairy eyeball?"

"Yeah." Toppy gave me a smug smile.

I thought for a moment. "Oh man. What about Angie?"

Toppy opened his mouth—and the front doorbell rang. "That's probably for you," he said.

"Me?"

We walked to the front door together. I opened it.

Hugh stood at the door in the gate, gripping the bars, staring at me, his face filled with misery. It was like seeing my man in prison. I ran to the gate.

"Get in here," I said, but neither Toppy nor I could find the keys. We finally clicked open the gate for the driveway and Hugh ran to me. Holding him in my arms was the best feeling ever. I kissed him, and the sound of the train whistle in my head stopped blowing.

I don't recall how we got in the house or how we stopped kissing and touching each other long enough to rip each other's clothes off. I do know I had the wise idea to try another bed out since mine hadn't been tidied up since we'd arrived. I also had to borrow condoms from my dad.

Safety first.

"I don't ever want to sleep with another man," Hugh said. "I hate that we have to use these."

I silenced him with kisses.

It felt so good to be with him, I couldn't stop kissing every inch of his body. He indulged me at first. I suppose he realized I was serious. I needed this.

"Please hurry," Hugh whispered finally, writhing underneath me. I took my time, however. I had pushed him from my mind, but my entire being had craved him.

My mouth reached his balls. His cock jutted toward him, but I held it in my hands. I adored his cock. For a slim man, he was huge. He was what we called a grower, not a shower. Relaxed, his cock looked small. Hard, it came to life in beautiful, big, enterprising ways. It was the sweetest cock I'd ever had.

He laughed as I licked and sucked his balls.

"You suck the way you eat food. You eat the potatoes first," he said.

When I took him into my mouth, the sensation made his eyes widen. His breath seemed to catch in his throat. He was bigger than I remembered. I shut my eyes so I wouldn't think about seeing him naked, in Bruce's bed.

My baby's hands stroked my head. "He never fucked me, Alex."

I stopped. I thought I would lose it. I kept my eyes closed and focused only on making him feel good.

"Get the damn rubber on," the most beautiful man alive said. "I only want to come with your cock inside me."

I lifted my head, aware only then that he was crying. I watched him sheath my cock. I wanted to lube his ass, but he begged me to lick him.

"Please suck me," he pleaded, his voice a soft mantra. I licked him and got him ready for me. He reached down between my thighs, keeping his hand on my cock. With his feet on my shoulders, he was able to keep a grip on me. I took my time until finally, I had to be inside him.

I leaned up and pushed myself inside. His legs slipped over my shoulders, his whole face changing. I fucked him slowly as my cock dipped more and more into him. I knew the moment I'd found his sweet spot. He fell apart, his legs falling to the bed as he screamed my name.

My name. Not anybody else's. I watched his lovely face, clamped my mouth over his. I fed him dick until he came, hard, his cock wedged between our slippery bodies. It was a good result, but not good enough.

Hugh loved to get fucked doggy-style. Until I'd met him, the position did nothing special for me, but I knew he loved it. I flipped him over and dragged him to his knees. I licked his ass up and down, back and forth. He tossed around like crazy on the bed, begging for my tongue, begging for cock. He went berserk. He was so wound up I wondered if he'd had even halfway decent sex with Bruce. I wanted to claim him, to devour him. He beat the sheets with his fists until I fucked him again. It was harder and deeper and somehow more intimate this time. I covered his back and shoulders with kisses.

"Fuck me, you bastard," he muttered, glancing back at me. I held his head in my hands and kissed him. I wanted him to come. I wanted him to come hard. I pulled out, frustrating him like crazy. I turned him over and told him to open his legs then ran my tongue over his hard abs and chest, my fingers focusing on his cock. I sucked him and plunged back inside him. His legs clamped around my waist. He kept up his aggressive muttering.

"That's it, fuck me. That's it."

I kissed him again, his mouth swallowing mine. I felt his hands move to my ass and he pushed me in deeper. I worked hard to keep up a brisk pace and kept at it. I felt his orgasm flush within him. It always stunned me when I could feel it. I'd never experienced that . . . *knowing* . . . with another man. His ass muscles clutched at me as his legs seemed to relax. He kept his hands on my ass cheeks, and I found myself begging God to let me make him come harder than he ever had in his life.

Hugh's release was better than if it had been my own. Only when I felt his breath of fire did I come, too, telling him I loved him.

"Don't ever leave me again," he said, tightening his hold on me.

For a long time, I lay on top of him, our kisses working their way into full-frontal ecstasy again. There was a soft tap at the door.

"Son?" Dad asked, cracking the door open. "We have to get going."

"Okay," I said.

I looked down at the man still pinned beneath me. "You

want to take a shower with me?"

"Okay."

We ran to the en-suite bathroom and showered quickly. I wanted nothing more than to be back in bed, naked with him. "Man, I missed you," I said, holding him tight.

"I missed you, too."

It didn't surprise me that as we threw on clothes, I got a text message from my brother.

Everything okay?

I texted back, *Never better.*

He sent me back a smiley face.

What about you, Zeca?

He texted, *Never better, but I miss you.*

I wrote back, *We'll be home soon.*

He rewarded me with a smiley face with an extra wide grin.

I turned to Hugh, who'd been reading over my shoulder. "If I ask you to marry me . . . soon . . . will you say yes?"

"Only if you get down on one knee."

I did.

"Yes," he said before I could even pop the question.

Outside our room, Dad was hopping around like a demented flea. "Are you getting married?"

"Yes," I said as Hugh collapsed in fits of laughter in my arms.

I had no idea what was so funny. "Why are you laughing?"

"Baby, your dad said things would work out. He even bet me they would."

"What was the bet?"

"I have to give him a game of *pétanque.*"

Half an hour later, I was sitting at an outdoor café at the Old Port, a charming seaside area of boats and fabulous fish restaurants, a glass of rosé in my hand. I watched the love of my life throw a little metal ball, or *boule*, in the French version of lawn bowling. I could see why it was called *pétanque*, however. That was the sound the metal balls made when they touched each other.

I couldn't keep my gaze off Hugh, and neither of us could stop smiling.

Hugh's father Jack sat beside me, his lover Jeremy on the other side of the table discussing fashion with Kathleen. It was an odd scene, but somehow fitting. I truly didn't get any sense of attraction between Dad and Kathleen. In fact, Dad didn't do any of the things he normally did with a woman. He wasn't showing off or peppering her with kisses.

Hugh and Dad were challenging each other, Dad enjoying a glass of *pastis* as the game continued. The late-evening sun started to set, and the village lights came on. Jack and Jeremy joined in the game, and pretty soon Dad lost interest. He was texting somebody, and he glanced over at me.

"I have to go, son. It's business."

Yeah, right.

He asked a local taxi driver who was snoozing in a chair if he could take him to Pampelonne. The grumpy driver agreed.

When Hugh came to the table and sat beside me, I slipped my arm around him. He leaned into me for a kiss. He was damn lucky we were in public, or he would have been in trouble.

Jack and Jeremy suddenly had some place to go.

"I guess you two have a hot date." Kathleen looked really depressed.

"Not really," I said.

"You don't think I'm hot?" Hugh's mouth turned down in a mock gesture.

"You're a beautiful fireball, baby."

He grinned at me.

"I just meant that we would love to hang out with you. Hey, is there some place we can have a nice meal and maybe dance?"

"You mean it?" Kathleen perked up instantly. "I know just the place."

Hugh had his car keys in hand and led the way to his convertible, parked under a huge plane tree. "You're going to love this place," he said.

We drove down to St. Tropez. The air was still warm, and for the first time, I truly loved the place. We found parking by the beach and walked into what looked like a wild, happening place. I soon learned Café de Paris was the in, in, *in* place. I stared at the antiques jostling for space with bunches of fake flowers in vases. There was a dance floor to the right of the entrance with a few hopefuls already shimmying to the canned music.

Kathleen seemed happy, and I suppose she should have been. She had some attention. Finally. I knew Dad was probably with Francesca and Kathleen was all alone. Hugh asked her if she wanted to dance as we waited to order drinks.

"Hell no," I said. "We'll both dance with her."

Her eyes sparkled as the three of us twirled around on the floor to Lady Gaga. Our antics got other patrons on the floor. After a few dances, we sat down, ordered drinks and appetizers, and Hugh and I took turns dancing with Kathleen, who had some pretty good moves.

"I wanted to be a ballerina," she told me at one point. "But I had Hugh instead."

"And I'm so glad you did."

We clinked glasses before a handsome Frenchman came over and asked her to dance. She was in his arms, her face tilted up to his, for several songs.

"I fucking want you," Hugh shouted over the music.

"Then let's get her and go home."

"No. I want to dance with you first. But not here."

"Wherever you want. I'm yours."

"Say that again," he shouted.

"I'M YOURS!"

"Yeah, you are."

He signaled for the waiter, handing him his credit card, then went to the dance floor. Kathleen apparently talked her new pal into coming with us to the next club, which turned out to be Chez Maggy, a hot gay club. I loved the place. Handsome men and women kissing each other. I reached my hand out to Kathleen, who looked amazed by it all.

Her date had disappeared.

"He asked for my number." She looked ecstatic.

"Good girl!" I kissed her hand, and she smiled.

We danced with her, and when she excused herself to go to the restroom, Hugh pressed me against the wall, kissing me.

I thought it was apt that the song blasting over the sound system was The Human League's 'Don't You Want Me.'

Kathleen came back, inserting herself between us. "I want to go home. I think I'm a bit tipsy."

As we left, I spotted her date. He was kissing another man. Poor, poor Kathleen. I distracted her, hoping she wouldn't notice, but she saw.

"It's the story of my bloody life," she said over the music, suddenly looking very old.

Chapter Six

We took Kathleen back to the villa I shared with Toppy. She looked quite impressed. She chose one of the empty rooms overlooking the pool and the gardens beyond it. We left her to it.

Toppy didn't seem to be home. The place was a bit messy. Not that I really cared, but I once again wondered about the alleged maid service. Hugh had one thing on his mind. Good thing we were so in sync. He steered me to our room, but I pushed him on the bed and got on top.

"But I'm clothed," he said. "Don't you want me naked?"

"In a minute. There are some things we need to discuss."

"Like what?"

I sat astride him, my hands pinning his to the bed. He gazed up at me.

"Like are we really going to get married?"

He grinned. "I bloody hope so. Do we need to discuss this right now?"

"There are some things you need to know about me."

"Like what?"

"My mother . . ." I shook my head. "No. I'm not going to blame her. It's just . . . it's just that I . . . I buried a lot of stuff from my past. I'm sorry I let it interfere with our present. I want to be with you."

"I know you do. And when I'm not quite so horny, I want to hear all about it."

"You don't love Bruce?"

He looked stricken. "No, I don't."

"You made out with him in front of me."

"He sucked your cock," he shot back. "*My* cock, really."

"Because I missed you."

He gave me a lazy smile. "He said you talked about me."

"Yeah. I've been doing a lot of that lately."

Our gazes held and I got off him. I undressed him as fast as I could, and he got a big, happy cock and a smile on his face — until we remembered we had no rubbers.

"Maybe Toppy has some in his room," I said. "Stay there."

He laughed as I ran off. I got to Toppy's room — and almost covered my eyes.

There was Dad, naked, his hairy ass in the air as he gave it to some woman underneath him.

I tried backing away but my man was right behind me, and I banged into him.

"Who the hell is that? It's not my mother, is it?" Hugh asked.

Toppy turned but didn't stop his actions. "Hey, guys. Meet Francesca."

The dark-haired woman's face appeared around his shoulder. She gave us a finger wave.

I waved back.

"Now scram," Toppy said. "Close the door behind you."

"We need rubbers," I said.

"Bathroom," Toppy gasped, and I closed the door.

I found his stash but couldn't wait to get Hugh to the bedroom. I picked him up and put him on the vanity. He brought his feet up to the edge, and I scrunched down and licked at his ass and balls. My favorite feast. His legs began to flail by the time I reached his cock. He gripped the edge of the marble top with his hands as I stroked his asshole with my fingers, sucked him. I nursed his ball sac in my hand, squeezing gently. They were my prisoners.

Hugh's body jolted when I tightened my hold. I released his cock and sucked his balls into my mouth.

"Put it in me, Alex."

He ripped open a condom foil and I slid it over my cock.

There was a small bottle of baby oil on the vanity. I snapped the cap open and squirted a bit onto him. He moaned as my fingers skidded over his hole. Now I couldn't wait. I moved right into him. In this position, my baby felt good and tight, his legs clutching my body to him. Man, I came almost the second I was inside. Our mouths collided and I held his ass to me with one hand, jerking on his cock with the other. He came fast, his tongue in my mouth, his heart pumping wildly when I finally put my lips to his chest.

I grabbed a few more rubbers, pulled out of him, threw him over my shoulder and took him to my room.

"It's my turn to fuck you," he said. I saw the baby oil in his hand. I shrugged. He was the first man I'd been comfortable bottoming for in a long time, and I realized now I craved it.

He ripped off the spent rubber and sucked me. He was also the first guy I'd met who didn't care about the taste of a cock after a rubber had come off it. He sucked me as if he'd been denied sustenance for weeks. Watching his fervor aroused me. He didn't take his mouth from me until I came a second time.

I wanted his cock back in my mouth, but he wanted to fuck me.

What could I do? The man owned me. I let him have his fun.

"Don't want you coming too quickly," he said.

I'd just come twice, so there was no danger of that. He was a great fuck. Hugh, like me, loved licking and kissing, and his huge cock was a thrill. He came deep inside me, and my motor had just started revving.

He pulled out of me and rolled to the side. I knew what he wanted. By now, I was on fire. I turned him over onto his knees, played with his ass with my fingers and tongue. He moved around, trying to get my whole face inside him. I slipped some pillows under his belly and slid a rubber over my cock. Then I tore into him. Hugh cried out for more. It was a blissful fuck. His ass was the finest I'd ever seen. With baby oil on his tight bubble butt, we worked up a slick and slippery sweat. I knew he was close again. I wanted to turn him over, but he wanted to come this way.

"Do it," he chanted.

I drew him up to his knees, my cock hitting all the way inside him. I threw the pillows from under him and brought his torso up. I was buried deep inside him, both of us kneeling on the bed, his body molded to mine, our mouths grasping for one another. When I gripped his cock, we came together, a sensational, blistering feeling that started, it seemed, from my ankles and careened up to the base of my spine. He cried out my name as he came in my hand, my cock erupting inside him.

We fell to the bed. I held him in my arms, his cock nestling against my thigh. I held him knowing I would never, ever let go.

He stirred early in the morning, waking me with kisses. In the near dark I told him everything, and even though he realized I was probably completely crackers, he still loved me. He touched my face with reverent fingers.

"Where do we go from here?" he asked.

"Back to Capri. I need you, but I also need Zeca. Will you come and live with me?"

"Of course," he said, passion dancing in his eyes as I stroked his cock back to life. I kept my fingers on him — until the bedroom door blew open.

I flew into instant protective mode and threw myself on top of Hugh, covering his body with mine. He gave a yelp, his hard cock wedged between our bellies.

I stared at the door, at the dark-haired woman in a slip dress. "Francesca?"

She nodded.

"What the hell are you doing here?"

She looked around, a bewildered expression on her face.

Toppy arrived beside her, zipping up the fly to his Bermuda shorts. "Angel?" he asked.

Hugh breathed heavily, trapped underneath me.

"This house," she said, her hand gripping the doorframe.

"Yes, it's a house." Toppy looked at her as if she was barmy.

"This is the house I clean," she said.

"You're the *maid*?" he asked, clearly stunned.

"Yes. I the maid."

"Then I suppose you'd better start cleaning," he said.

Hugh looked up at me. "Sweetheart, I see where your insanity stems from."

I would have responded except that Francesca screamed at us to get out of bed so she could wash the sheets.

Dad dragged her away, giving us some privacy to shower and change. It was barely seven and the day was already turning out to be wacky.

"Put your swim trunks on," Hugh said. "We're going to the beach."

First, we had to get through the strangest breakfast on record.

Dad made eggs, toast, and coffee whilst Hugh and I set the table. Kathleen picked a few oranges from a tree in the garden and sliced them up.

Francesca went mad. She screamed at my father in Italian. Her promise that she would soon separate most of his body from a certain small part to which I knew he was attached seemed to set him into panic mode.

"We're leaving today," he said.

"Today?" Kathleen started to cry. "But I'll be all alone."

"Come with us," Dad urged. He sure seemed to specialize in dingy dames.

I couldn't get him alone long enough to ask him how he planned to deal with Angie once we got back to Capri. We threw our stuff into our suitcases and followed Hugh and Kathleen back to their house so they could pack, too.

Afraid of letting Hugh out of my sight for even a minute, I followed him to his bedroom. I was worried he would change his mind about tying himself to my crazy *vita*. Next to his bed, on the bedside table, was a photo of the two of us. He blushed when he caught me looking at it.

I picked it up. We looked so happy in the photo. I'd blown it all away.

"I'll make it up to you," I said. "I'm taking you back to that restaurant in the middle of all those lemon trees. I'm gonna get on both my knees and beg you to spend the rest of your life with me."

He stepped into my arms. "Prove it."

I would have given him an immediate demonstration, since I'm a show-don't-tell kinda guy, but my dad burst into the room.

"We can't get on a flight until this evening." He looked very uncomfortable, but I couldn't understand why.

"What's wrong?" Hugh asked him, his arm around me as if to steady me for bad news. "It's not like it isn't beautiful here."

"Francesca is Angie's sister." Dad threw his hands in the air. "Who knew?"

Hugh and I stared at him.

"We need to get out of here *now*." Toppy looked borderline hysterical. "Angie's on her way here. I'm afraid she's going to set fire to my guys."

"Your guys?" Hugh gazed at my father then at me.

"My baby makers!" Dad was near the boiling point.

"Dad, running away won't help. Let's just sit down with the two sisters and talk to them calmly and — "

"Are you *crazy*?" Toppy shrieked. "Angie put fingernails in my coffee and spat in my food!"

"She did *what*?" Hugh asked.

"We're leaving in fifteen minutes," Dad said. "Be ready. I have a plan."

He rushed out of the room again.

Hugh moved away from me.

"Are you having second thoughts?" I asked. I was actually wringing my hands.

He turned back and stared at me. "Getting my suitcase, darling. But since we're on the subject, I do think your father would benefit hugely from heavy doses of psychotropic medication." He jumped when Toppy stormed in again, throwing his arms around.

"All solved, all solved. I booked us on a luxury cruise back to Capri, hitting all the hot spots along the way. Sorrento, Pompeii, the Amalfi Coast." He pointed at Hugh. "Start packing."

"Aye, aye, captain."

Toppy stared at him. "Captain. I like that. I need a new hat."

He ran out of the room again.

"I take back everything I said." Hugh reached under his bed, dragging out his suitcase. "Nothing but electroconvulsive therapy can possibly help him."

We scrambled to get out of St. Tropez in time to catch the cruise ship. Hugh's father promised to return the rental car in Paris. I think he was relieved to have Kathleen off his hands for a while. So much so that he dropped us off at the harbor and even bought Toppy a Greek fisherman's hat from a souvenir store.

The yacht was magnificent. She was a skippered, two-hundred-thirty-foot vessel with rooms for thirty people. They were mostly couples . . . I got the feeling many of them were gay since all I saw were hot guys drifting around the deck. I had my own hot guy, and I wanted to mark my turf as soon as possible.

"I feel like we're going on our honeymoon," I told Hugh, holding his hand as we clambered onboard.

We had a very nice cabin with plenty of space. I locked the door and insisted we try out the bed immediately. I didn't get much of an argument from Hugh. He stripped down to his swimsuit, my hands roaming his body before I shed everything except my own swimsuit. He pushed me onto the bed, pulling down the scant fabric separating us.

Hugh sucked my cock as I lay back, listening to the onboard noises. Toppy rapped a couple of times on the door, but I was too far gone, and so was Hugh. His fingers snaked inside me as he sucked. He spread my legs after removing my swim trunks, and his face disappeared between my ass cheeks as he licked and sucked. I stared out the porthole at the blue sky when he finally came up for air, but then his mouth moved to my nipples, sending me into a frenzy. He slid two fingers inside me, taking my cock in his mouth. I came, clutching his hair.

I wanted to suck him, but he shook his head. "We need sun."

Unhappily, I agreed to get back into my swim shorts. We went on deck and found Toppy, who glowered at me. Beside him on her deckchair, Kathleen sipped a tropical drink and flirted with a guy beside her.

"This is a gay cruise," Toppy hissed.

"Still, it's beautiful, isn't it?" I asked. "I bet you guys can do with a breather. Aren't you going to get into your swim trunks?"

"Hell no!"

Geez, Toppy, you're not that cute, I wanted to say, but he *was* getting a lot of admiring glances. He seemed petrified.

Toppy wasn't the only one. I'm not exactly chopped liver, but Hugh is spectacular. The guys onboard circled him like starving wolves.

"He's my husband," I said. Often.

"There's no ring on my finger," Hugh said, holding up his bare hand. Oh, he was enjoying my agony and the ecstasy of all that attention.

I was lucky, however. Hugh isn't a natural flirt. The man just had a healthy ego. Toppy and I are both possessed of raging jealousy. Zeca is the only one in our family who is even halfway normal. Well, at least he was until he met Antonio.

Our cruise was a nonstop stroll through visual delights. Toppy got used to guys ogling him. In fact, he enjoyed having a captive audience that laughed at all his jokes and endless impersonations.

Hugh and I spent a lot of time alone, sun-baking naked on a private deck, watching dolphins swim as we made love. Our port stop in Pompeii was a welcome respite from the sea and cocktails. Our yacht anchored and we took a walking tour through the ancient city destroyed by volcanic eruption. I was particularly interested in one of the rooms alleged to be an ancient brothel.

Well, it sure got *my* motor running. I wanted to make love to Hugh on one of the stone beds, but he was worried we'd get caught.

He took my hand. I had to run to keep up with him. In our matching white pants and white T-shirts, I felt we'd somehow gone back in time. A bare shoulder here or there and we could have been young Italian lovers in togas, which I knew they wore back then. The late-afternoon sun fell down on the ruined city. My heart almost broke when we saw the remains of a tethered dog that had died when the lava flowed right down the street and covered him. Having been tied up, he'd had no chance of escape, but then there weren't many survivors at Pompeii.

Hugh hurled himself into my arms.

"When we get a dog, promise me we'll never tie him up."

"I promise," I said, kissing him.

The others were walking toward us. It was time to go back to the ship.

Hugh was a sun worshipper. He loved to fuck every morning in full sunlight. Well, he loved to fuck any time of day. And after a hot romp in our cabin, he liked a hearty breakfast then some solid sunbathing. I didn't care what we did. I just thanked God for every second I was near him.

I was amazed Bruce didn't call him, but Hugh kept reminding me he'd dumped the guy.

"He's a professional gambler," I told him. "He doesn't like to lose."

"But he did lose," Hugh said. "I belong with you."

We lay around in the sun, talking idly of the future. He started tanning his toned torso, lying on his back. I stared at his beauty. Before I could indulge in a taste test, he said he wanted lotion on his back and turned over. Of course I complied. My hands had a mind of their own. I squeezed some of the tropical-scented cream onto his back, his skin soft and hot. My hands worked on his shoulders, kneading their way down. I took my time until I got to his ass. My hands settled between his cheeks.

Hugh stiffened. "You can't. Not here," he insisted, but I found his asshole and stroked until he was short of breath.

"Get on your knees," I said. He did as he was told, and I was pleased to see his cock was rigid. I didn't think anyone was watching and wouldn't have cared. I wanted to suck his cock in the sun.

I put my mouth on his ass, his skin tasting of coconut lotion and the sun. I inhaled his beautiful, masculine scent. He was on his knees, his ass rising to meet my greedy tongue. His moans turned me on, and I slid underneath him.

"Oh God," he said as I lay between his legs, waiting for him to feed me his cock. He angled himself over me and fucked my face. It wasn't the best way to get all of him in my mouth, but I worked some magic with my tongue. Hugh went crazy as I hooked my finger around the base of his cock and sucked him in all the way.

He fucked my mouth gently, then more aggressively. He needed release. I reached between his ass cheeks and slid two fingers inside him. His whole body shook as he gave me what I wanted. My nose was buried in his hard, flat belly as he ripped his way into an explosive orgasm, filling my mouth. I swallowed as best I could. I heard footsteps, but he was too far gone to stop.

"Hot," I heard a voice say, then the footsteps went away.

My sweetheart scooted between my legs, and his cock stayed hard and very wet. I wanted him badly.

"Not here," he said. "I want to fuck you in our cabin."

Fine by me.

Two days later we were on the Amalfi Coast, the weather blustery. We'd made contact with Zeca and Antonio. Toppy instructed them to shut the café for a week. This wasn't an unusual time to close shop; in fact, it was perfect since it was the low season. It was, however, unusual for Toppy. I don't think he'd ever closed the place. Even on Christmas.

Antonio protested that his mother had arrived on the island and would have nothing to do. She wanted to keep the place open.

"Tell her to meet us in Naples, we'll have fun," Toppy insisted. She didn't want to, however. She wanted to keep the place open and had plenty of staff. Everyone seemed happy with the arrangements.

Zeca assured me that once I met her, I would love Antonio's mother. "She's so . . . sane," he said. In the meantime, we were going to enjoy some free time together. Antonio insisted there was plenty of room for all of us in his apartment in the city.

Zeca kept calling my cell phone. We got excellent signals since we all had satellite phones. Hugh and I couldn't wait to reach Naples. He wanted pizza. I wanted to buy wedding rings.

Antonio promised to help me. He said he knew a great jeweler.

Zeca promised Hugh he knew the best pizza joints.

When we docked at the harbor in Naples, I hugged my twin. He looked fantastic. We'd never been apart this long, and the small niggles of anxiety left me.

Kathleen surprised us all by deciding to stay onboard the yacht.

"They've asked me to work as their executive chef, and not *all* the guys are gay," she said. "I'm gonna give it a try."

Dad wanted to stay onboard too, since he and Kathleen had been the stars of the tour. Everybody thought they were an item and neither of them dissuaded anybody of the idea.

"It could be worse," Hugh said to me. "She could have fallen for Bruce."

They said they would meet us in a week in Capri. I

hugged my dad, who said we should take a week in late spring and go to Madrid since gay marriage was legal there. He kept staring at Kathleen. It surprised me to see that he seemed really smitten.

"I keep expecting her to act bonkers, but so far, so good," he said.

Kathleen hugged me and Hugh. Son of a gun, I was going to miss them both. But the ones I needed, Hugh and Zeca . . . I had them right with me.

Dad hugged me again. "I love you, son."

"Love you, too, Dad."

They waved us goodbye.

As we strolled with our bags toward Antonio's apartment, he warned us that men holding hands was okay in Naples, but ardent face sucking was not. Yet at every opportunity, he seemed to lean into my brother for a kiss.

Hugh's cell phone rang. He checked the readout.

"Shit," he said. "It's Bruce."

"Is that the other guy?" My brother moved into instant protect mode. I loved him for it.

"Let me handle this," I said.

Hugh handed me the phone.

"What the fuck?" Bruce howled. "I want to talk to Hugh."

"He's busy right now, being my boyfriend."

"You two won't last a month."

I laughed. "Wanna bet? Oops. What am I saying? You never like to bet on things you can't win. So don't bet on it, asshole. And don't ever call us again."

I hung up on him.

"So macho," Antonio said, but he grinned at me.

"My hero," Hugh said. I kissed him. I didn't care if it was okay or not.

Zeca stepped in and hugged me.

At Antonio's apartment, Hugh and I admired the wonderful old relic of a building and our view of Naples from the window. "We're in such a beautiful part of the world," Hugh said, kissing my face. "Since you came back to me, every moment is like a new revelation."

Yeah. Being relentless had sure paid off.

"I want you to fuck me in this bed," he said, bouncing up and down on it.

"You know I will." I smiled. "You can bet on it."

Antonio took us out to their favorite patisserie for coffee. A noisy backgammon tournament was in full swing across several tables. The players were elderly women, and you never heard such swearing. Hugh and I exchanged grins as the game turned explosive. Antonio checked his watch.

"We must go to the jewelers," he said, kissing my brother goodbye.

"I'll bring pizza home. I'll wait for you in bed," Hugh promised.

He got a kiss for that.

Antonio and I walked away from them and I felt like pieces of me were left behind, like Hansel and Gretel's breadcrumbs.

He led me into a tiny, wonderful little store, where he helped me choose wedding rings.

Antonio examined a tray of expensive-looking cufflinks nestled in blue velvet folds. He held up a pair. "I think I've settled on these for your brother. What do you think?"

My lip curled involuntarily. "You're buying my brother . . . your beautiful lover . . . *cufflinks*?"

"I'm not really a ring guy, Alex."

"If you say so."

I stared at the rings in my hand. They felt good and heavy. Solid. They felt real. You might even say . . . relentless.

"What's that supposed to mean?" he asked.

I shrugged. "Have you asked my brother how he feels?"

"I . . . er . . ." Antonio put down the cufflinks. He scratched his chin. He picked up another pair. "How about these?"

"They're even worse. They're so old-fashioned. Has my brother said he wants a pair of cufflinks?"

"Not in so many words. But he didn't say he *doesn't* want them."

"Hmmm."

"What's this mean? This *hmmm*?" Antonio put the second set of cufflinks down.

"You're nervous," I said. That shocked me. "You're sweating."

"Of course I'm sweating." He slapped his hand down on the glass, making the tray of cufflinks jump. He also left a wet paw print on the glass. "I love Zeca more than anything but . . . two men," he wagged his finger, "shouldn't get married."

"Why not?"

"It's all right for you," he said hastily. "I'm not judging you."

"Are you ashamed of my brother?"

"My God! Of course not. He's my angel!"

"Then buy him a ring, you big dope."

"I . . ." He stared at the rings.

"Zeca and I are the same size. Here. I'll try some on, and you'll see how nice they look."

Antonio's mouth hung open. "I like that one." He pointed to the one I'd selected for myself.

"Oh, go on," I said. "Take it."

He held it between two fingers. I couldn't tell if he thought it was the Holy Grail or a bomb about to go off in his face. "I wanted to get him cufflinks," he said finally.

"And he would wear those with what? His T-shirts?"

"They're beautiful. I like cufflinks."

"Hmmm."

He stamped his foot. "Stop saying that."

"Buy him the ring. You can call it a cufflink. And since we're talking about cufflinks, they come in pairs. You should have one, too." I passed him the matching ring for the one in his hand.

"Cufflinks are nice!" he insisted.

"They're stupid," I insisted.

He held the rings in his hands and slid one of them onto his finger.

"Very nice cufflink," I said. I glanced at the store owner, who seemed quite entertained by our discussion.

"Our best 'cufflink,'" he said.

"Hmmm." Antonio let out a long sigh. "Dammit, this feels good. I don't want to take it off." He kept staring at it. "I never thought this would happen for me, Alex. I accepted my life would not be like other people's because I was gay. We are such a repressed group of people. I lived with it. I . . . I adjusted to it. Now . . ." He blew out another sigh. "I can think of it as a cufflink until I get used to the idea. You don't think people will think I'm a big gay man because I have a wedding ring on, do you?"

The storekeeper held up his right hand. They wore them on the right hand in Europe. He wore a wedding ring, and I was pretty certain he wasn't gay.

"Get the cufflink," I said. "You're the sexiest mofo I ever met, apart from Hugh. You're very macho. I think it's the sexiest thing in the world, a wedding ring on a man in love."

Antonio's eyes glazed over. "Oh . . . he will look so beautiful naked in his . . . cufflink." Antonio glanced at the shopkeeper. "Can you polish the one for Zeca?"

"I can polish both of them." The man held his hand out for them.

"You want my cufflink?" Antonio held his hand to his heart.

"Of course he wants it," I said. "Besides, Zeca has to put it on your finger."

We made our purchases. I gripped the small bag holding the box with my rings, and Antonio held his cufflinks with an iron grip. He wore a big, goofy grin on his face all the way home.

"Won't Zeca be surprised?" he asked.

I grinned.

"You don't think he'll be surprised, Alex?"

"I think he will be over the moon, Antonio."

When I'm right, I'm right.

Back in the apartment, our lovers had pizza, salad, strawberries, and chilled champagne waiting for us. The look on my brother's face when he saw his cufflink brought tears to my eyes. He was so knocked out, he couldn't speak.

I had to nudge Antonio to put it on him.

Hugh loved his ring, too. I dragged him to our bedroom. I wanted to make love to him wearing nothing but our rings.

"The champagne will get warm," he muttered between kisses.

"I totally dig warm champagne," I said.

With shaky hands, I took off his clothes. His skin tasted of coconuts, sun, love—and me.

His hands moved to my face. I wanted our first time as betrothed partners to be long and languid, but that would have to wait. He begged me to fuck him, and I did.

"I got myself ready for you," he said. "I have lotion all over my ass. I couldn't wait for you to come home, Alex."

My cock slid into him, and across the square from our open window, I heard the sounds of laughter. I heard the sounds of rolling dice and the voluble swearing of the old ladies.

I laughed and laughed. I'd just rolled the dice in the game of love.

And I'd won.

ZECA'S CAPRI LIMONCELLO

Ingredients
    10 lemons
    1 (750-ml) bottle of vodka
    3 ½ cups water
    2 ½ cups sugar

Directions

Using a vegetable peeler, remove the peel from the lemons in long strips (reserve the lemons for another use). With a small, sharp knife, trim away the white pith from the lemon peels; discard the pith. Put the lemon peels in a 2-quart pitcher. Pour the vodka over the peels and cover with plastic wrap. Steep the lemon peels in the vodka for 4 days at room temperature.

Stir the water and sugar in a large saucepan over medium heat until the sugar dissolves, about 5 minutes. Cool completely. Pour the sugar syrup over the vodka mixture. Cover and let stand at room temperature overnight. Strain the limoncello through a mesh strainer. Discard the peels. Transfer the limoncello to bottles. Seal the bottles and refrigerate until cold, at least four hours. Keeps up to one month.

YOU MAY ALSO ENJOY THE FOLLOWING FROM EXTASY BOOKS INC:

Relentless Obsession
A.J. Llewellyn

Excerpt

Over the next couple of hours, I tried to make myself useful and adjusted to Uncle Toppy bossing me around. I found I was most helpful to him and Zeca by collecting glasses, spoons, and dishes. I discovered that my cousin had an unhealthy phobia about running out of spoons. He seemed obsessed to me.

Toppy showed me the way they liked to wash the glasses, cups, and spoons by hand. He made me wear only one glove because he said I needed one hand free to rinse and dry. They couldn't wait long enough for the dishwashers to go through a load. The plates and cooking pots and all the utensils went through a heavy wash cycle in detergent that smelled like lemons. That was nice. Other than that, frankly, I found the morning traumatizing.

"It's my own brand," Toppy told me when I mentioned the lemon soap. "I sell it in the café."

I'd done two loads when he finally gave me some time to talk to him right after the morning rush.

"We have a fifteen-minute window," he said. "Then bedlam strikes again. What are your plans, kid?" We walked outside the café and parked ourselves at one of the suddenly empty tables.

"I don't know, Uncle Toppy." I was exhausted. Not from my work in the kitchen but my life in general. I'd thought I'd been so careful, saving my money, investing it . . . I still had my apartment in West Kensington, in London, and I'd rented it out. That would bring me some income. Waking up and not rushing to the studio set in Ealing was a reality that was just starting to hit me.

For the first time in twelve years, I had no schedule, and I was floundering. The difficulty was in trying to decide what to do with the rest of my life. I'd had plans to live and write in Greece, but my apartment building had been totally destroyed in the riots last year, and I'd had no idea.

"I've been working sixteen-hour days, and I was led along by a disreputable real estate agent who told me the building had sustained some damage," I said. "We stayed in touch by text and cell phone calls. We even Skyped, and she was charming. I believed her. She kept billing me for repairs of all kinds and told me tenants had fled. I believed that, too. I'd stayed abreast of the horrible problems in Greece, particularly Athens."

Uncle Toppy was staring at me. He let me ramble.

"I kept sending her money, but when my bank in Athens contacted me asking when I was going to follow the government's instructions and demolish what was left of the building, I flew straight to the city to check on things."

"When was this?"

"Two weeks ago, two days after I'd finished my last episode of the series."

It had hit me harder than I thought. I expected to maybe get rid of some stuff, take my time moving to Greece. I'd left one apartment empty for me to move into.

My parents, who lived in London, had persuaded me to

rent my flat fully furnished through a company that rents to tourists looking for an 'at home' experience. My mother had handled everything with surprising ease. And now . . . I was without a home. I'd promised my London digs to the rental company for the next two years.

Telling Toppy all of this was devastating.

"So this realtor was scamming you the whole time?"

I nodded. "Her husband's an attorney. I met them through my dad."

"He's a plonker," Toppy said. He had every right to think so. We'd had a rough history we had to agree to overlook the day we started working together on the soap. I was the son of Toppy's ex-wife's brother. The ex-wife I knew had once kidnapped Alex and Zeca and almost got them killed in a train wreck. It had ruined our wonderfully tight, close-knit family existence.

My parents still acted weird about Toppy. After the kidnapping, they had never wanted family dinners . . . or holiday celebrations. But for me, there was something about Toppy and the twins I couldn't let go of. I became an actor because Toppy was one. He'd mentored me. He'd been good to me. But ultimately, he had always wanted to be a restaurateur and here he was.

He'd quit the show a few years ago and never looked back. I realized now that he hadn't been lying to me whenever we talked on the phone. I could see the café was damned hard work, but as I watched him and Zeca flitting around all morning, I could tell it was their passion. They loved what they were doing.

"I don't think you made a mistake investing your money, and it's possible you can get compensation from the Greek government . . . eventually," he said. "It'll be years before they sort out the mess. In the meantime, I can help you get a good European Economic Community attorney. Those guys are cleaning up all the scams, but I don't want it to define your existence, okay?"

"Okay." Suddenly I felt better. Toppy had a way of just saying things, making it all seem sensible, reasonable.

"You did good, kid. You invested your money like we talked about. But for future reference, invest where you can keep your eye on the prize."

Yeah, he was right about that.

He called out to Zeca for two more coffees.

"You seem so happy working," I said. I still couldn't get over that. I thought he was over here living the good life.

"Work is love made visible." Toppy grinned just as Alex crossed the terrazza over to us. He looked great, too. He seemed so pleased to see me, and within minutes, Zeca was with us, the four of us 'gas bagging,' as my mother would have called it, over coffee. They heard my whole sorry saga, since Toppy made me repeat it all.

"You can stay at the house with me." Toppy had a thoughtful look on his face. "You can sit around like a dilettante and write, or . . ." His voice drifted off.

"Or?" I asked.

He kept stirring his coffee. "Zeca's room is free. He's moved in with Antonio. Hugh and Alex have a room. They sometimes use it to get away from their pesky patrons."

"They're not pesky," Hugh said.

"Yes, they are," Toppy said. "Let's just call a spade a shovel here. I read some of their Yelp comments. Those little cretins."

Alex, Zeca, and I laughed.

"Now, Marius, I believe in the value of hard work," Toppy said. "You'll learn more about life working here than you ever did on that stupid TV show."

I opened my mouth to protest, but he said, "No, no, don't thank me. Now listen. I don't need rent from you, but I could really use your help here. You're a natural, kid."

Yeah, a natural klutz. Didn't he see me stumble around here like Blind Freddie?

"You can wait tables. You'll get paid, of course. You'll get great tips. You will meet a guy. A great guy. Both my Zeca and my Alex met their husbands right here working at this café."

"Really?"

The twins nodded.

Toppy went on. "Oh, and you can have your pick of lunch or evening shift."

I wanted to say that I wasn't a waiter. I liked being waited on, but I saw the hope in my cousins' eyes.

"Erm . . ."

When I caught both twins mouthing the word lunch at me, I said, "I'll take lunch."

"Good." Toppy seemed so happy. "That gives you the rest of the time to write and figure out if that's what you want."

Toppy's lady-friend walked by us. I saw the way she looked at him. I wasn't sure if it was desire or a passion to kill. He leered at her. I saw the worried looks the twins exchanged.

But Toppy, oblivious, extended his hand to me. "We got ourselves a deal?"

"Yes."

We all shook hands.

"Welcome home," Alex said. I knew he meant it.

As I picked up my cup to enjoy the last, delicious sip of coffee left in it, I spotted a tall, dark and sexy man jogging toward us. My God, he was gorgeous. Dressed head to toe in black, his hooded sweatshirt slipped back, and I glimpsed his golden features. He was so hot I missed my mouth with the coffee cup and liquid ran down my chin.

For one brief second, our gazes held, and I could swear he smiled at me, but it was a kind smile. And then he passed us by.

And suddenly I felt I had been right to come here. A door had closed on my dreams, but a window, just a little one, had opened in my mind, and a small breeze carrying the scent of lemons wafted over me . . .

ABOUT THE AUTHOR

A.J. Llewellyn is the author of almost three hundred published gay romance novels. A.J. lives in California, but dreams of living in Hawaii. Frequent trips to all the islands, bags of Kona coffee in the fridge and a healthy collection of Hawaiian records keep A.J. refueled.

A.J's passion for the islands led to writing a play about the last ruling monarch of Hawaii, Queen Lili'uokalani. A.J. has written a non-erotic novel about the overthrow of her kingdom written in diary form from her maid's point of view.

A.J. never lacks inspiration for male/male erotic romances and has to prise fingers from the computer keyboard to pursue other passions: collecting books on Hawaiiana, surfing and spending time with family, friends and animal companions.

A.J. Llewellyn believes that love is a song best sung out loud.

Webpage: www.ajllewellyn.com
Facebook: www.facebook.com/aj.llewellyn
Twitter: www.twitter.com/ajllewellyn
Email: ajllewellyn@gmail.com

OTHER TITLES BY A.J LLEWELLYN

Available at eXtasy Books
  Temptation Eyes
  Night School Vampire
  The Fetish Café
  The Crimson Cat
  Island Heat

  Fawnskin
  Fawnskin
  Frenzied

  The House Of Driscoll
  The House Of Driscoll
  Precious Blood

  Black Point
  Black Point
  Back to Black Point
  Black Point Revisited
  Black Point Surrendered
  Black Point Christmas
  Black Point Forever

  Blood Eclipse
  Blood Eclipse
  Rapture
  City of Blood
  Apocalypse

www.ingramcontent.com/pod-product-compliance
Lightning Source LLC
Chambersburg PA
CBHW071627140626
46555CB00021B/953